SIREN
Publishing

MARLA MONROE

Ménage Everlasting

A Place in Their Hearts

RIVERBEND, TEXAS HEAT 7

A Place in Their Hearts

Rayna takes in a mother cat and ends up with kittens. When she takes them to the local vet, she gets more than an exam. He's interested in her, but he comes as a pair. Kenny and Jay have plans for Rayna that include lots of hot loving.

Kenny and Jay have always wanted a woman to share between them but could never agree on one until now. They both want Rayna and are sure she would be perfect to make a family with.

Rayna is worried about there being two of them. She doesn't want to cause a rift between them and even though they say they're fine with sharing her, she's leery of the arrangement.

Kenny and Jay work together to teach her that where one might be busy the other is always going to be there for her. To Rayna, she is getting the best of everything. What's in it for them?

Genre: Contemporary, Ménage a Trois/Quatre, Western/Cowboys
Length: 35,248 words

A PLACE IN THEIR HEARTS

Riverbend, Texas Heat 7

Marla Monroe

Siren Publishing, Inc.
www.SirenPublishing.com

DEDICATION

As time passes, I miss my mom and dad even more. The love they showed for each other will always be my guide. I love you both so much.

ABOUT THE AUTHOR

Marla Monroe has been writing professionally for over thirteen years. Her first book with Siren was published in January of 2011, and she now has over 75 books available with them. She loves to write and spends every spare minute either at the keyboard or reading. She writes everything from sizzling-hot cowboys, emotionally charged BDSM, and dangerously addictive shifters, to science fiction ménages with the occasional badass biker thrown in for good measure.

Marla lives in the southern US and works full-time at a busy hospital. When not writing, she loves to travel, spend time with her feline muses, and read. Although she misses her cross-stitch and putting together puzzles, she is much happier writing fantasy worlds where she can make everyone's dreams come true. She's always eager to try something new and thoroughly enjoys the research she does for her books. She loves to hear from readers about what they are looking for in their reading adventures.

You can reach Marla at themarlamonroe@yahoo.com, or
Visit her website at www.marlamonroe.com
Her blog: www.themarlamonroe.blogspot.com
Twitter: @MarlaMonroe1
Facebook: www.facebook.com/marla.monroe.7
Google+: https://plus.google.com/u/0/+marlamonroe7/posts
Goodreads:
https://www.goodreads.com/author/show/4562866.Marla_Monroe
Pinterest: http://www.pinterest.com/marlamonroe/
BookStrand: http://bit.ly/MzcA6I
Amazon page: http://amzn.to/1euRooO

For all titles by Marla Monroe, please visit
www.bookstrand.com/marla-monroe

A PLACE IN THEIR HEARTS

Riverbend, Texas Heat 7

MARLA MONROE

Chapter One

Rayna looked at the pregnant cat curled up in the wheelbarrow in her shed. The storm brewing outside howled past the little structure. It would be raining soon. The momma cat looked scared and thin despite her bulging belly.

"Well, hell. Looks like I'm going to be a grandma, and I'm not even married. Easy, kitty. I won't hurt you, but you can't stay out here in this storm. We're going inside." She located an empty box and slowly approached the skittish cat.

She wasn't sure if it was her soothing voice or that the cat was just too exhausted to put up a fight, but she allowed Rayna to pick her up and relocate her into the box. She didn't even growl, just cowered when Rayna picked up the box and shoved open the shed door to rush across the backyard to her back door.

Once inside, Rayna settled the box on the floor about a yard from the gas logs. Even though it was early April, the weather was cool, and the rain coming made it a damp cool. She had the gas logs going.

"Give me a second to find you a towel to cushion the box."

She'd need to think of a name other than momma cat. She'd need to feed it, as well. She had tuna fish and some milk that would work fine until she got cat food.

"Here you go, momma." Rayna shoved the towel as carefully as she could underneath the cat's bulging stomach. "I'll get you something to eat now."

Thirty minutes later, the cat was pleasantly purring after having demolished the can of tuna and a small bowl of milk. She made biscuits, kneading the towel beneath her as she closed her eyes.

"Glad you enjoyed it, kitty cat. What can I call you?"

The momma cat was a multitude of colors much like a patchwork quilt. Oranges, tans, black, and gray blended into a furry blanket. Rayna smiled. She had the perfect name for her little friend. Patches.

"What do you think? Will you be happy with Patches, girl?"

The cat opened her eyes to mere slits and meowed once then closed them again and settled into a perfect circle, complete with tail curled around beneath her chin. Rayna ran one hand lightly over the soft fur and was glad she'd checked the shed to be sure everything was fine inside before the storm hit. It promised to be a big one.

Sometime around midnight, while the storm raged outside the house, Rayna checked on her new addition and found that one had turned into five. Momma had given birth to four gorgeous-looking kittens. One marmalade orange, one solid black, and two that looked just like their mom.

Rayna cooed and congratulated Patches on a job well done. She'd take them to the vet on Monday to be sure they were all fine and healthy. Momma cat curled around her litter as they nursed, purring the entire time.

"You did good, Patches. They're precious."

Momma cat just continued to purr with her eyes closed.

* * * *

Rayna waited her turn at the veterinarian's Monday morning. Since she worked from home, she could afford to take off a few hours to get the cats checked out. Patches was obviously nervous and protecting her kittens with a paw over them.

"It's okay, little momma. I won't let anything happen to your babies." She'd transferred her to a larger box for transporting her to the vet.

One of the cats she'd noticed in the office walked over and sniffed the box then walked around Rayna's legs before sauntering back through the door leading to the back.

"Miss Collins. The doc is ready for you." A vet tech stood in the open doorway leading to the back. "Do you need me to carry them for you?"

"No thanks. I've got them. Momma cat is a bit nervous." Rayna stood up and crossed the floor to the open door and entered the exam room.

"What do we have here?" The tech opened the box and smiled. "Pretty kitties. Momma looks a bit malnourished."

"She is. I found her last night in my storage shed and took her inside. She had the kittens sometime before midnight."

"I'm going to take momma to weigh her. Be right back." The tech gently extracted Patches from the box and disappeared through another door.

"Mommy will be right back, sweeties." Their high-pitched whines jerked at her heart.

When the tech returned with Patches, the cat leapt into the box with her babies.

"Here you go. She only weighs five pounds."

"That's bad?"

"Yeah, for her bone structure and paw size, I think the vet is going to want to put her on some sort of supplement. He'll be in soon." The tech drew up medications and set out various tools the vet might need.

Rayna sighed. She hoped Patches would be okay. Though she'd never thought of having a pet, she was already attached to the new mother. Finding homes for the kittens wouldn't be all that difficult she was sure. There were only four of them.

The opposite door opened, and a handsome man stepped into the room wearing surgery-green scrubs. He was at least six feet tall with a runner's body, trim and strong. His dark brown hair was cut short and a light sprinkling of facial hair covered his lower cheeks and chin, with a well-trimmed mustache. She was sure her mouth fell open before she managed to regain control and stop looking into his warm chocolate-brown eyes.

"Hi, I'm Dr. Kenny Long." He held out his hand. "I hear you've been blessed with a litter of kittens."

Rayna shook his hand, warm and firm, then twisted her fingers together. She'd never been nervous around other people before, but for some reason, she felt uncomfortable with the attraction that had instantly fallen over her for the good-looking doctor.

"She had them sometime before midnight last night. I found her in my storage shed."

"She's very underweight. The kittens look good though. Nature tends to take care of them at the expense of the mother. I think with the right food and good care she'll recover nicely though."

"The tech mentioned something about a supplement."

"Right. It's an appetite stimulant and high-calorie paste you can squeeze on her paw so she'll lick it off, or if she likes the flavor, you could probably just squeeze it on her food." He felt her belly and checked her ears, nose, eyes, and mouth. "I'm going to clean her ears and apply flea medicine. It won't hurt the kittens, and they'll benefit, as well. Also, I'm going to trim mommy's claws so she won't accidentally scratch one or you."

"Dr. Long. When is she safe to get her spayed?" Rayna didn't mind the initial kittens, but she didn't want any more of them.

"Call me Kenny. I'm not formal. Normally I'd say in six weeks, but it's going to depend on when she gains up to a safe weight and is healthy again. We'll check her in six weeks to see where she stands.

You can bring them all in, and we'll vaccinate the kittens then, as well."

She watched as he gave Patches something in a syringe then gave her two injections before clipping her nails. He smiled and rubbed the cat down her back then scratched her behind her ears.

"You're ready to go. It was great meeting you, Rayna. I'll see you in six weeks unless you need me before then. My tech will give you the supplement to get you started. You can buy it and Momma cat food at the local pet store. Feed her as often as she'll eat."

"Thanks, Doctor…um…Kenny. I appreciate it."

Rayna carried the box out to the front desk to make another appointment and pay. The tech gave her some handouts on caring for new kittens, a tube of the supplement, and a coupon for cat food. She thanked them and carried Patches and her kittens back to the car. She'd take them home then return to buy the necessities she'd need for her new cat.

She decided it was best to take the cats home before picking up the supplies she'd need to care for the new addition to her family. She returned to town and headed straight to the store.

While she was loading up on cat paraphernalia, Rayna wondered why she'd been so attracted to the cute vet. She hadn't gotten that kind of rush from any of the other men she'd dated. It boggled her mind that she'd turn into a bundle of hormones over the man. Yes, he was good looking, but so were most of the men she'd been out with. None of them had caused her pussy to flutter with need like Kenny had.

I must be feeling my age. I'm only thirty, but I guess that's old to not be married already.

The truth was she'd never met anyone she wanted to spend the rest of her life with before. Now, she could see her future with this man.

I don't really know him. He might already be married or in a relationship.

She hadn't noticed a ring on his finger, but that didn't mean anything these days. A lot of men didn't wear wedding bands for some reason. It had always made her wonder if they were truly committed to being married.

Once she'd managed to make a good dent in her checking account, Rayna loaded up her car and returned home where Patches had gotten out of the box sitting a yard from the fireplace and lay stretched out between it and the gas logs. She looked happy and comfortable, so Rayna didn't bother her. Instead, she unloaded the car and set up the litter box in her laundry room where she'd placed a temporary box with shredded paper overnight.

I'm going to like having a cat. I can already tell. The house feels more alive with her in it even though she's only sleeping.

Once everything was in place and the new food in the brand-new food bowl, Rayna returned to her office to get to work. She handled insurance questions for an insurance company. She was one of hundreds of people across the nation who fielded questions from beneficiaries. She logged into her account and settled the headpiece on her head to answer her first call.

In between calls, her mind kept returning to Kenny. She liked the slightly scruffy look with the beard and mustache that was just barely there. It made her want to scratch her nails over it and feel it against her cheek. She groaned and squeezed her thighs together. She had to stop thinking about the man.

I'm obsessing over my veterinarian. That's crazy.

Well, it was better than obsessing over her OBGYN. That would be sick. No, she'd take the vet over her doctor anytime. She was sure the attraction would fade over time. She wouldn't be seeing him again for six weeks. She'd be back to normal by then.

Maybe. But he'd be a good image to fantasize about when she fiddled with her BOB at night. She could easily see him looking down at her from his position over her. Maybe she'd have her hands on his chest or maybe she'd have them wrapped around his neck. Rayna shivered and cut off the image before she soaked her panties again.

I can think about him, but he's off-limits.

Or was he?

Chapter Two

Kenny had a difficult time concentrating the rest of the day after meeting Rayna. Her curvy body and thick, loose curls of bright red hair remained in the back of his mind. She'd smelled of something rich like vanilla and cream. It was a good thing he didn't have any emergencies or problematic patients that day.

I'm obsessing about a woman I just met. What's up with that?

He could still see her mesmerizing green eyes and luscious pink lips. She hadn't been wearing any makeup that he could tell, and the soft sprinkle of freckles across her nose was cute. Then her body. Lord, just thinking about those soft curves had his cock rock hard. He hadn't been this turned on since he'd been a rutting teenager full of hormones and the hots for anything in a skirt.

Jay will tease the crap out of me when he finds out.

Normally it was Jay who went after the women they dated. He and Jay had been sharing their women since they'd met in college. The other man had lacked the skill to keep a relationship going at the time while Kenny tended to get too serious too fast. They'd been the perfect combination, each helping the other to rein in their weak areas.

Nowadays, they didn't date quite as much since they'd grown weary of losing interest after a few weeks. They hadn't been able to find the one perfect woman for them in Riverbend or the surrounding communities. It weighed heavily on them.

He thought about Rayna and wondered if she might be someone they could enjoy getting to know. He already knew he was attracted to her physically. He'd liked that she'd brought the momma cat and babies in to be checked. That proved she was sensitive and probably a really nice woman. Maybe, when she brought them back at six weeks, he would have thought up a good way to ask her out. He doubted Jay would have any objection. The man loved first dates.

Later that evening, Kenny returned home and found Jay locked in a battle of wills with Chester, their mastiff. It looked like Chester was hogging Jay's favorite chair and refused to get up.

"Look, boy. If you don't get up, I'm going to have to make you get up, and neither one of us wants that."

"Ha," Kenny said. "He doesn't care if you move him by hand or not. You're the one who won't like it with your back."

"Furry devil dog. I swear. He was perfectly happy on the couch, but as soon as I walked in after my shower, he jumped up and ran over here. He does it to me on purpose." Jay settled his hands on his hips. "You tell him to move. He'll listen to you."

"Chester. Give Jay back his chair, or he'll pout all night."

The big dog yawned then slowly got down off the chair and returned to the couch. Jay growled.

"How are things out in the shop?"

Jay made furniture and custom cabinets for several contractors in the area. He loved working with his hands and was in high demand.

"Good. I finished the Harvey's breakfast table. I'll work on finishing the cabinets for the big house they're building outside of Smithville in a few days. I'm glad they weren't in a hurry."

"Thought any more about if you're interested in the Lexington project?"

One of the city council members wanted to build a new library. The old one was barely large enough for six to ten people at any given time, and they had nowhere to add books. They wanted Jay to build the shelves and do the woodwork around the new building once it was finished.

"Yeah. I'd love to do it. I just wonder if I'll get bored building shelf after shelf after shelf."

"Break it up some. Work on the front desk and other things in between shelves. I think it would be neat to have a library with your work in it."

"Yeah, maybe."

"I met someone today at the office. She's pretty and really sweet."

Jay's head whipped up and around. "You did? Is she new to the area?"

"I don't know. I've never seen her around, but that doesn't mean she's new. She lives out on Shiloh Road close to the Murphys," Kenny told him.

"Why did she come in today?"

"She found a momma cat who delivered last night. She wanted to be sure they were all healthy. The momma was very malnourished, but the kittens look healthy."

"She's a good person then. Can't fault someone who loves animals enough to take them in and take care of them." Jay sat forward with his elbows on his knees.

"I was thinking about inviting her out to dinner when she comes back in six weeks."

"Six weeks? That's a long time to wait." Jay liked to forge ahead and wasn't one to wait.

"I don't have any reason to call her up to ask her out. I'm not sure how else to approach her when there's no reason for me to see her until then."

"Call her up in a few days and ask after the momma cat and kittens. Just follow up to be sure the momma cat is eating well."

"Maybe."

"Do it. Don't wait six long weeks. Call her in a week. That should be plenty of time for the momma cat to show some improvement."

"All right. I'll call next Monday and ask her out for coffee. How's that?"

"Perfect. Now tell me all about her," Jay said.

"She's got fiery red hair that curls and reaches just past her shoulders. They're big curls that you can twist around your wrist. Her eyes are summer-grass green, and when she smiles, they light up like a Christmas tree. She's about five feet, four inches and has the softest curves you've ever seen. Man, her ass is drool-worthy. I wanted to squeeze it so badly when she walked out of the exam room."

"Fuck, I'm sprouting wood just listening to you talk about her."

"She's got the cutest trail of freckles across her nose. I bet she has them in other places, as well."

"What do you think? Is she someone we might see for more than a few weeks?"

"I don't know, Jay. She might be."

"Awesome."

"Don't go getting your hopes up. You know how tough it is when it doesn't work out."

"I know, I know, but I can dream."

* * * *

Rayna couldn't stop thinking about the handsome veterinarian. He dominated her dreams at night and her thoughts during the day. She struggled to concentrate while she worked. Checking in on Patches and her kittens didn't help matters.

Patches seemed much more relaxed and was eating well. The kittens already looked less like miniature rats and more like furry kittens. She couldn't wait for them to open their eyes and start moving around more.

Six weeks. That was a long time until she saw Kenny again.

I've got to stop lusting after the man. He's bound to have a steady girlfriend. Someone as handsome as he is probably has several.

Her cell phone rang, startling her as she recorded her latest call for work. She didn't recognize the number but answered anyway.

"Hello?"

"Hi, is this Rayna?"

"Yes. Can I help you?"

"This is Kenny, your vet. How are Patches and the kittens doing?"

"Oh, hi." Rayna's stomach jumped as if full of baby rabbits, and tiny goosebumps erupted down her arms. "Patches is doing great. She's eating a lot and really being a great momma kitty. The kittens are fat and roly-poly. I didn't expect a call to check on them. Thanks."

"Actually, they were just an excuse to call you and ask if you'd be interested in coffee sometime." Kenny's voice had dropped to a slightly deeper note.

"You're asking me out?" Rayna couldn't believe it. Her.

"Yes. I'd like to get to know you better. Are you interested?" he asked.

Rayna wished she could see his face. She could tell a lot about a person when they were talking by looking at their face. It was one of the things she liked least about her job, no face-to-face conversations.

"Um, sure. I'd like that."

"Great. How about tomorrow morning at ten? I don't have any appointments from then till one that afternoon."

"Okay, sounds good. Where should I meet you?"

"How about the diner? They have great coffee and pie."

"Pie?" Rayna laughed. "You must have a sweet tooth."

"I sure do." Again his voice deepened. It tickled along her nerve endings.

"Okay. See you tomorrow at ten."

"I look forward to it. Bye, Rayna."

Before she could say good-bye, he'd ended the call.

A date. She had an actual date with Kenny. Sure, it was only coffee, but it was still a date. Now she had to stress over what to wear. Did she even have anything nice enough without being too dressy for a coffee date?

Rayna had to stifle the urge to run and check her closet. She had to concentrate on work and do her job. She needed to put Kenny out of her mind.

Right.

As soon as she could cut off her calls for the day, she updated her log and files then raced to her bedroom and the closet. Choosing an outfit wasn't her strong suit. She'd never been a girly girl and collected dressy clothes like her sister, Amber. If it had been Amber going on the coffee date, she'd have had to choose between lots of nice-looking outfits. Rayna only had three to choose between. None of them really appealed to her, but he'd seen her in her jeans and a sweatshirt only days before. Surely anything better would be in improvement.

She finally settled on a forest-green pair of slacks paired with a green and tan blouse. It was the best she could do.

Rayna pressed the outfit and hung it on the back of the door to be ready for her ten o'clock meeting. Date. It was a date.

When was the last time I've been on an actual date? Has it really been a year?

Well, working from home didn't offer many opportunities at meeting men. Mostly she met them at the grocery store or department store. Now she could add meeting one at the veterinarian's office to the list. It was an improvement, right?

Thoughts of the man's trim body and capable hands had her body softening and her pussy quivering. She could just imagine what those strong hands might feel like on her body. Would he get hard just being around her as she got wet from being around him?

God, she sure hoped so. Rayna wanted him to like her. She sure liked him. He had to be kind and giving to be a vet. She wanted a strong man who was able to give her the hard, dirty loving she craved while still being sensitive to her feelings. Would he have both qualities? Could she find herself falling for him?

Hell yeah, she could. Already her heart beat fast just thinking about him.

I'm in trouble. Thinking along those lines when I haven't even been out with him yet is dangerous.

But Rayna liked a little danger with her man.

Chapter Three

Kenny checked the time for the tenth time. He'd arrived early and secured a table toward the back to give them some privacy. He'd already ordered his coffee but wasn't going to presume to order hers yet. Another five minutes and she'd be there. Unless she was one of those women who were always fashionably late.

He grinned. Nothing like waiting for a woman. He'd gladly wait for Rayna. She would be worth it. He was almost sure of it. Something about her sweet cooing over the momma cat and kittens appealed to him.

The waitress checked on him again. "Still waiting?"

"Yeah, but I'm early. She probably won't get here for another five or ten minutes."

"Never seen you nervous before. She must be something else."

Evelyn had waited on him most every time he'd been in the diner for lunch. Sometimes, when business was slow, he'd go in for a piece of pie and coffee, as well.

"She's really nice. I haven't seen her around before, so I'm thinking she might be new here."

"Maybe. What does she look like?"

Kenny described her, and Evelyn smiled. "I think I've seen her in a few times. Don't think she's too new though. I know I saw her around Christmas last year."

The bell over the door rang, and Rayna walked in, hesitating just inside the door as she looked around. Her face lit up when she spotted him. Kenny rose to meet her when she reached the table.

"It's good to see you. I love that blouse you're wearing."

"Thank you." She allowed him to hold her chair as she scooted into the table.

"It brings out the green in your eyes."

She blushed so that her cheeks turned a rosy pink. He loved that she blushed. The freckles across her nose stood out with the heat in her face. He could imagine that her chest would turn pink, as well, since the blush seemed to creep down her neck.

"Would you like coffee?" Evelyn appeared at the table seconds later with a winning smile across her face. She winked at Kenny, but he was sure Rayna hadn't noticed.

"I'd like a Diet Coke instead of coffee, please."

"I'm glad I didn't order your coffee now," he told her.

"I don't drink a lot of coffee. I normally drink Diet Coke when I go anywhere." Rayna's eyes sparkled with laughter.

"Thanks for meeting me here. I wanted to get to know you without it making either of us uncomfortable like a first full date might."

Rayna thanked the waitress for her drink and took a sip. "Thank you for asking me. I was a little startled to hear from you."

"Why? You're a lovely woman, and I'm single. I would have asked you out sooner if I'd known you. Are you new in town?" Kenny asked.

"No. I've lived here about six years. I don't get out much. I work from home."

"What do you do?"

"I field calls from customers who have insurance and billing questions concerning their health care. I work for a company that contracts out the services all of the country to people who work from home." Rayna smiled. "I already know what you do."

"Do you like your work?"

"Love it because I can do it from home, or even if I wanted to travel somewhere else."

"I love my work, too. I like animals and have always wanted to be a vet."

"Do you have pets outside of your business?" she asked.

"Two dogs and four cats. Then there are the two office cats."

"Office cats?"

"They live at the office and serve as greeters and the occasional blood donor if need be."

"I guess I have a part-home, part-office cat now, as well." She grinned.

"I'm glad Patches is doing well. Don't expect her to gain much weight for the first three or so weeks. Everything she's taking in is going to feed those babies. She'll plump up once they get to be five or so weeks old."

"She's so sweet. She purrs and purrs for those kittens."

"What do you like to do when you're not working?" he asked.

"I like working in my yard. I have a small garden every year, and I like to read."

"I like cooking and hiking. My roommate keeps a garden for us. I'm not always home enough to look after it. As for reading, I only seem to read articles concerning work."

"I've gone hiking before and enjoyed it, but it's not safe to go by yourself."

"We'll have to go sometime."

As they talked, Kenny couldn't keep his eyes off of her. She was so pretty with her hair held back with some kind of pen or something. He could easily imagine running his hands through her hair as he kissed her. Jay would love holding it as he took her from behind. Yeah, he was already fantasizing about filling her with his cock as his friend took her sweet ass.

Rayna had luscious curves and a rounded belly. He'd love to rest his head there and take a nap. There was nothing as appealing to him as a full-figured woman who wasn't ashamed of her body.

"Are you the only vet in your clinic?" she asked.

He snapped out of the trance he'd been in and smiled. "Yep. Makes for some long days sometimes, and I'm on weekend call for emergencies. There's a vet in the next town who sometimes fills in for me if I want to go somewhere and can't be accessible."

"That's nice. I would think always being on call would be stressful."

"It can be, but I love my job, so it's usually not a drudge." Kenny smiled as he held his coffee cup for the waitress to refill it.

"Would you guys like a piece of pie?"

"I'd love a piece of your pecan." He nodded toward Rayna. "What about you?"

"Not for me. I ended up eating a late breakfast. Thanks."

"So, I'm thinking a second date. How about dinner at my place Saturday night?"

* * * *

"And she agreed?" Jay asked.

"She did. She hesitated though. I think she was unsure about jumping right into the more intimate atmosphere of our house, but I wanted to include you without it being uncomfortable in public this early."

"How do you think she'll take it that there are two of us and we come as a pair?" Jay asked.

"I'm not sure. She hasn't been out much in public from what I can tell, so I'm not sure if she even knows about the threesomes here in Riverbend. It might be sticky, but I really like her, Jay. She's sweet but has a wicked sense of humor."

"I tried to find a Facebook page for her, but either I don't know what she calls it or she doesn't have one."

"Not everyone has social media like we do, man."

Jay shook his head. "It's almost laughable that she wouldn't when she makes her living working from home and on the computer."

"There are firsts for everything."

Jay shrugged. He couldn't wait to meet Rayna. Now he had to think of something good to cook for her. He loved to cook, and if he hadn't loved working with his hands as much as he had, he might have thought about being a chef.

"Any preferences that you picked up on for food?" he asked.

"No, I should have asked her about her favorite food. Sorry, man. I was having a really difficult time listening and not drooling all over her. She's so perfect for us."

Jay chuckled. "Falling hard isn't a good idea, man. You know how you get over a woman. Take it slow."

"This from the man who can't stick with one woman long enough to really know her."

Jay sighed. His friend was right. After four or five dates he normally lost interest in the woman. He despaired that they'd ever find the perfect one for both of them. They preferred sharing a woman since their personalities complemented each other and pleasuring a woman was so much fun with two of them. Seeing the woman you loved explode with pleasure when you weren't overcome by your own from time to time really was a rush.

"Maybe she'll be the one, and I don't get bored. She sure sounds perfect from what you've described so far."

"I think if this dinner date works out, we should all go hiking the next weekend," Kenny suggested.

"Great idea. I'll pack a picnic lunch I can carry in a backpack. You should carry the blanket and all of the water we'll need. I don't want her to have to carry one."

"I like that idea. I'll pick out an easy trail that will show her some good sights but not be too difficult for a beginner. I don't think she's hiked in a while."

Jay sat back on the chair and thought about the possibilities dating would bring to them. He wanted a family one day. Maybe a son to teach woodworking but then he might want to be a vet like Kenny. He didn't mind one way or another. He wasn't in a hurry for children. Getting to know their woman and making her feel wonderful would fill up several years he was sure.

He wished he knew more about what she looked like. His cock was already hard just at the thought of a luscious woman to seduce and tempt with all of the pleasure he and Kenny could give her.

Their relationships in the past had always ended after four or five weeks because he grew bored and wasn't as into them as Kenny was. He was surprised his friend hadn't given up on him and found a woman of his own instead of sticking with him to share one. Sharing provided so many possibilities, plus there was always someone around to take care of her if the other one was gone.

That's why Kenny still wants me as part of a threesome. He's gone so much for work I would always be around to care for her.

Jay jumped up and walked into the kitchen to look at what they had on hand so he could make a grocery list of the things he might need from the store for their Saturday night dinner. Once he had his list, he told Kenny where he was going and headed to the store.

It didn't take him long to fill his cart. While he was determining which bell peppers to choose, a woman's buggy hit against his.

"I'm sorry. I wasn't paying attention." Her sweet voice did something to his body as he jerked his head up.

"No problem. I'm in the way because I'm trying to pick out the perfect pepper." He smiled at her.

"Well, save one for me." She smiled back

Jay couldn't believe he'd met someone at the grocery store he wanted to explore when they already had someone coming for dinner. What were the odds of that?

"I'm Jay. I think we should at least exchange names since we've had a bit of a crash."

Her deep-throated laughter stirred his cock. He wanted to push her up against the produce shelf and ravage her mouth. It took every bit of restraint he had not to moan with the thought. She was magnificent with her pretty red hair and those light green eyes. He could easily imagine running his hands all along her curves.

"I'm Rayna. It's great to meet you."

Jay froze. Could it really be the same woman that Kenny had met? What were the odds?

"I think you've met my roommate, Kenny." He waited to see her response.

"Um, yes, I have." He could see the blush starting at her neck and rushing to her cheeks.

"So tell me, what do you like to eat? I'm cooking for you Saturday."

"You are? That's awful nice of you to cook for your roommate and his date. He must not be much of a cook."

"Nope. He's the outside grill king. I'm the kitchen chef." He hoped he hadn't screwed things up.

"I don't really have many food preferences. I'm not much on olives, guacamole, or anchovies."

"Noted. I don't plan on having any of those in the meal. Do you like wine?" he asked.

"I do. I have a glass or two on occasions."

"White, red, or blush?"

"I'm not picky."

"Wonderful."

Jay grabbed up two peppers and set them in the cart. "I better let you finish your shopping. It was really good to meet you, Rayna. I look forward to Saturday night."

Her answering smile waned a bit but didn't completely disappear. Maybe everything would be fine after all. He still had to tell Kenny that he'd met her.

Wonderful.

Chapter Four

Rayna wasn't sure how she felt as she drove home from the grocery. She normally went at night to avoid the daytime crowd. Of all the people she could have run into, what were the odds it would be Kenny's roommate? What made things even worse, she'd been instantly attracted to him before she'd known who he was.

God, how am I going to go to dinner at their house feeling attracted to both of them at the same time?

There's no way she'd ever cause a rift between friends. If it continued, and if she wanted to date both of them, Rayna would have to back away from them. She'd finally found someone she was attracted to, two somebodies, and they were best friends. It all added up to disaster.

After she'd put away her groceries, Rayna settled on the floor next to the box with Patches and her kittens. She loved watching the pretty momma take care of her babies. It made her think of the handsome vet and his gorgeous brown eyes. She could look into them all day. He'd been nice and a complete gentleman during their coffee date, but she'd sensed that his emotions ran deep.

Then his roommate came to mind. The man was devilishly handsome and so outgoing. She'd been instantly aroused by the way he'd looked at her as if she were his favorite dessert. A girl could get used to that.

Which was why she was worried. Maybe she should cancel the date before anything went any further. That didn't sit well with her, but she was concerned about how the three of them would interact with the way she'd reacted to both men.

What am I going to do if I like both of them?

She guessed it would depend on if she liked Jay more than Kenny and if Jay even acted like he was interested in her.

I could have sworn he looked me over before he knew that I was going on the date with his roommate.

There was nothing she could do about the situation now except wait and see how it played out. For all she knew, Jay had a girlfriend and would only be around long enough to finish cooking the meal.

Rayna couldn't help thinking about how good Kenny looked in a pair of scrubs. The arms stretched to accommodate his muscles while the shirt stretched across broad shoulders. She supposed handling large animals required that he stay in shape. She could imagine him having washboard abs that she could run her fingers over.

I'd like to run my tongue over them, as well.

That wasn't going to happen anytime soon though. She didn't mess around on a first date. She wasn't counting the coffee meet-up as a real date. They still needed to get to know one another before anything resembling sex played out.

"I can't believe I'm thinking about sex when I hardly know the man."

She needed to think of something else other than the handsome vet. She still had nearly an entire week before she had dinner with him at his place. That was more than enough time to dampen down her physical reaction to the man. She needed to concentrate on work and Patches for now.

* * * *

"You're fucking kidding me." Kenny shook his head. "What did she say when you introduced yourself?"

"Not much. She seemed okay. I think it startled her, but I don't think she was upset." Jay continued unloading the groceries. "I like her. She's sweet and was hot in those shorts she had on."

"She was wearing shorts?" Kenny sat at the bar as he watched Jay put away the food.

"Yeah. Not short shorts, but they showed off her pretty legs. I bet she will be great at hiking like you said."

"So you like her?"

"Yeah. I do."

Kenny sighed. "I wonder how she'll take it when you join us for dinner."

"I'm betting she'll take it in stride. It won't be until we both take her hiking that she'll begin to wonder about it. I mean I cook a meal for you guys, so it would only be natural that I eat with you, right?"

"I want this to work a lot more than I thought I would. I mean I don't normally get this worked up over a date this early on."

Jay nodded. "She's special. I don't know what it was about her, but I really liked her. She just seemed so natural, you know, not put on when we talked."

"I think she's the one, Jay. Let's pray she'll accept us both. We need to contact some of the others when we get ready to take her out together. I'm sure they will be glad to all go out on the same night so that she sees that there are other threesomes around."

"Good idea. I hadn't thought of that." Jay folded up the paper bags and thrust the plastic ones in the bag holder before leaning back against the counter.

"We're going to need all the help we can get if she turns out to be the one we fall for. I know I'm already attached to her. She's sweet and funny. She loves animals. What's not to love about her?

"Haven't found anything yet. We'll just see how the night goes this weekend. What time is she arriving?" Jay asked.

"Six. I thought we'd have a drink before dinner then, after eating, watch a movie."

"Sounds good. I'll have the food ready by six thirty."

"The scene is set."

* * * *

Rayna's subconscious wasn't cooperating because her dreams that night included both men as they seduced and made love to her, despite her determination to stop thinking about them.

Kenny held her loosely in his arms as he kissed her. His tongue teased along hers then dove in deeper to learn every private space there. Then he sucked on her lower lip and nipped it.

As he kissed her, Jay ran his mouth down the back of her neck, pulling her hair to one side so that he could lick and nip along her neck and shoulder. The two men ravished her body with just their mouths before she felt herself being moved and laid back on a mattress as soft as downy feathers.

They seemed to divide her body and slowly removed her nightshirt and panties as they licked and nipped their way around until she was a writhing mess of arousal. How could she be dreaming this when she'd only just met the two men? It would seem that her libido didn't have a time limit on when it was appropriate to dream about sex.

Kenny placed opened-mouthed kisses down her jaw line and over to her ear, where he sucked on the little lobe before dropping down to her neck. He spread kisses over her neck and chest as he slowly slipped southward to her exposed breast.

Jay nipped and bit along her jaw line, leaving little wisps of pain as he went. Each small bite sent shock waves down her body, where her pussy reacted by growing wet with her desire. Two men so different in how they touched her and she'd not even been with them to know how they made love. Her body had ideas of its own.

Both men took a breast in his mouth and began sucking and biting at the heavily aroused nipple hardened for their pleasure. Rayna dug her fingers into their hair to hold them at her breasts as they sent shock wave of electric vibes all through her body. Jay broke free of her hold and made his way lower to spread her legs and settle there.

He blew a warm breath over her moist center as he spread her pussy open before him.

She could hear his indrawn breath a second before he plastered his mouth over her pussy to lick her from bottom to top and back down again. His stiffened tongue probed inside as deeply as he could get, and then he sucked on her clit until she saw stars.

Before she could recover, Jay got to his knees and spread her legs wide apart to fit his body between them. Kenny kneeled next to her head so that his thick cock now stood erect next to her face. All she had to do was turn her head and she could reach him with her mouth. His taste exploded over her tongue when she licked at the tip, where a drop of pre-cum had gathered. His groan matched her own as she reached out to lick again. This time he fed her his dick with one hand.

Rayna groaned around him so that the vibrations traveled up his stalk. Kenny jerked in her mouth. She laved his long cock with her tongue then sucked him as far down her throat as she could manage and swallowed around him. He dug his hand in her hair and groaned.

The next thing she knew, Jay had his hard dick centered at her slit and was pressing inward. He moved slowly and deliberately as if afraid of hurting her. She thrashed her head back and forth, losing Kenny's dick from her mouth as she did.

Jay pulled back and drove deeper as she screamed out his name. He stilled inside of her then set a slow, steady pace where he tunneled in then pulled out, rasping at nerve endings with every thrust. Rayna was sure she'd go crazy with the slow pace. She wanted him to fuck her hard and fast, but he wasn't going to be hurried.

Kenny turned her head back to him and his hard cock. She drew him back into her mouth and sucked while teasing him with the tip of her tongue around the edge of the rounded cockhead. He fisted his hand in her hair as she swallowed around him once more. The deeper she went, the harder he seemed to grow in her mouth.

Jay's dick tunneled in and out of her tight, wet cunt, growing faster with each thrust. Rayna was sure she'd explode with the way he scraped across every nerve ending inside of her. She'd never felt so touched like she did now with both men moving inside of her.

She moaned around Kenny's cock when he began to lose his rhythm and cried out as warm rivulets of his cum coated her throat and mouth. She swallowed as fast as she could but still couldn't manage to get it all. Some leaked from her mouth as she gasped for air. The man collapsed beside her, running his hand over her chest to collar her throat before kissing her.

Suddenly her arousal jumped up the ladder as Jay slipped one finger down to brush her clit as he thrust in and out of her overheated body. He threw back his head and cried out her name as hot streams of cum filled her body, even as he pinched her clit, making her squeeze against him even tighter. When it was over and the three of them lay atop each other, Rayna wondered how it could all feel so real though it could only be a dream. She'd never even been out with Jay, yet she was sure of his touch and how he'd react. Since it was only a dream, she refused to let it make her feel embarrassed that she'd included Kenny's roommate in it. She didn't have to tell him about it. Right?

Chapter Five

The weekend arrived before she knew it. Rayna had worried over the upcoming dinner date all week once she'd realized that she was attracted to Kenny's roommate as well as him. She promised herself that she'd make sure to only pay attention to Kenny if Jay was there part of the night, as well. She'd acknowledge his skills as a cook and let that be it. She hoped.

The kittens had their eyes open now and were moving around a lot more. They mostly crawled since they couldn't really get their legs under them yet. Patches was an amazing momma kitty. She spent time outside of the box only a few feet away as she relaxed by the gas logs, but she was always near them. Even when she ate, she checked back with them every few bites. Rayna was pleased to see that she was slowly putting on a little weight. She knew that it would pick up some once the kittens were no longer feeding from her as much.

After taking a shower, she spent over an hour going through outfits until she finally settled on a pair of khaki slacks with a soft forest-green sweater with a rounded neck that gave just a hint of cleavage. It was one of her dressier tops. If she was going to go on more dates with Kenny, she'd have to improve her wardrobe so as not to be embarrassed with what she wore.

Working from home meant she mostly wore warm-ups and jogging pants or shorts around the house. No one would see her while she talked with customers on the link with her computer. Now she had someone to dress up for. Maybe. She didn't need to get her hopes up until she had this date behind her. It was only their first real date.

Who am I kidding? I really like Kenny. The only problems that might happen are if he decides he doesn't like me or if I like him and his roommate too much.

That little issue hadn't gone away since she'd last thought about it. She really did like Jay, as well. There'd been something about him when they'd met over the peppers that had hit her right between the eyes. His wit and the way he'd come clean that he was Kenny's roommate had endeared him to her.

She glanced at the clock by her bed and groaned. She only had another thirty minutes to get over to their house. She still hadn't put on any makeup. Rayna hurried through that by only adding what was necessary to keep from looking washed out and grabbed a light sweater and her purse before telling Patches good night and not to wait up for her.

I'm getting too worked up over this. I need to step back in case it doesn't work out.

That was easier said than done. She hadn't been on a real date in over a year. This was like a mixture of her birthday and Christmas all wrapped up with a great big bow.

She pulled in behind a black Jeep Cherokee and cut the engine before sitting there for a few seconds to calm her nerves. When she climbed out of her SUV, the front door opened and Kenny smiled and waved to her.

"Hey, come on in. I'm running behind. I ended up going back to the office to see about an emergency." Kenny took her sweater and ushered into the large living area that was separated by a large tiled island where Jay was working on the meal.

"Hey, Rayna. Great to see you again. I'm going to entertain you while Kenny takes a shower."

"Oh, okay. Thanks."

Kenny squeezed her hand. "I'll only be a few minutes."

"Have a seat," Jay said, indicating the stools across from where he worked on cutting up a salad.

"Thanks. What's for dinner?" she asked.

"A variation of baked spaghetti. It's nearly done in the oven, and I'm finishing up the salad now. I'll put the bread in when I get the main dish out. How about a glass of wine?" he asked.

"Sure."

Rayna's stomach rolled. She still thought Jay was cute, and arousal bloomed through her body just talking to him. Where did that leave her and Kenny?

I'm doomed to be single all my life. First I can't find one man to tickle my fancy, and now I have two I really like and can't choose because they're best friends.

She plastered a smile on her face despite how she felt at the moment. She was going to enjoy her date tonight and deal with whatever happened once it was over. If Kenny asked her out again, she'd figure something out to turn him down.

Damn!

"Here you go. It's a Lambrusco. I hope you like it."

She took a sip and nodded. "It's good. I bet it's going to go well with the baked spaghetti."

"Thank you. I think it will. So, Kenny said you worked from home. Something to do with health insurance, right?"

"That's right. I answer questions about their policies and direct them to physicians in their network. That sort of thing."

"Are you on the phone a lot, or is it a feast or famine sort of job?" he asked.

"It's pretty steady. I rarely get more than ten minutes between calls, if that."

"Wow. That would make me nervous to have someone always right there waiting on me." Jay pulled out the main dish then shoved a foil-wrapped loaf of bread into the oven after it.

"What do you do, besides cook?" she asked with a forced grin.

He cocked his head then smiled. "I do woodworking and cabinetry. My office is the workshop behind the house."

"Really?" She could see that he liked what he did from the way he smiled as he told her.

"Yeah. I like working with my hands. That's why I said it would make me nervous if someone was always hanging over me waiting for me to finish something."

"I get that. If I were working with my hands on something, I'd end up cutting a finger off with that kind of pressure. The worst I do is accidentally hang up on someone when I'm nervous about a call."

Jay chuckled. "Having been on the other end of a call about a piece of equipment that I can't get to work right, I can tell you that is frustrating, but not life threatening."

"Oh, I've gotten some threats before when what I tell them isn't what they thought it should be. I'm very happy that I work on a recorded line and no one can locate where I am after one of those calls." Rayna shivered.

"I can imagine. So what do you like to do outside of rescuing momma cats and working?"

"I love the outdoors. I keep a little garden and love to hike, but I haven't been in a while. It's not safe to go alone, and I don't really know many people here. That's a hazard of working from home, as well."

Jay nodded. "Kenny mentioned that you might like to go on a hike. That will be fun. I'll fix a picnic lunch for you guys."

"Thanks. If we go, I'm sure it will be great."

This is getting too hard to keep up. I really like Jay. How am I going to deal with how I feel about Kenny's friend when I like Kenny just as much?

"Looks like everything is ready." Jay pulled out the bread. "Here, you can take the wine to the table for me while I set everything else out."

Rayna placed the wine bottle on the table then sat where Jay indicated. It was then that she realized that there were three place settings. He was planning to eat with them. God, could the night get any more difficult?

"I'm back. Sorry about that." Kenny walked over to where she sat and kissed her on the top of the head. "Someone's dog got wrapped up in some barbwire, and it took a good hour to cut it all off of him. Fortunately they kept him calm so that he didn't rip himself up too badly. Just required a few stitches and a collar to keep him from chewing on them."

"Oh, poor thing. That's that Elizabethan collar we always called the cone of shame." Rayna felt sorry for the poor pooch.

"Yep, that would be the one." He sat on one side of the table while Jay finished setting out the salad and salad dressings.

"I hope you guys are hungry. I made enough for an army. We can always freeze whatever we don't eat for later." Jay poured more wine in his glass then passed it to Kenny. She noticed he poured only a half glass.

"Dig in, guys." Kenny passed the salad bowl to Rayna, and they began filling their bowls and plates with the meal Jay had cooked.

Rayna slipped a bite into her mouth and closed her eyes as she moaned with delight.

"This is amazing. I love it." She couldn't help but praise the man for his culinary skills. "You should have been a chef, Jay."

"It was a hard decision, but I decided I liked woodworking a little more than cooking, so that's what I do full time and the cooking is a hobby now." Jay smiled at her.

"He built all the cabinets and bookshelves in the house," Kenny told her.

"Really?"

"He bitched the entire time because it took so long." Jay chuckled as he spooned up more spaghetti.

"Did not. I only fussed after the fourth week of waiting for you to say it was ready."

Rayna enjoyed their byplay and how they seemed to get along so well. It only drove home the fact that she couldn't break them up by choosing one over the other. Her heart broke at the realization that she was going to have to refuse a second date.

"Hey, where did that frown come from?" Kenny touched her elbow.

"Sorry. Nothing. I was thinking about one of my last calls and how they were so upset over the changes to their policy. The elderly really get to me when they are paying for coverage and it turns out to not be what they really needed."

"I can imagine. You must be really good at your job to worry about your customers like that."

"This was delicious, but I'm stuffed. Can I help with the dishes?" She started to stand up, but Kenny stopped her.

"Nope. We're doing the dishes, or, rather, the dishwasher will do them. Why don't you have a seat over there on the couch, and we'll watch a movie once we've cleared the table."

"Really, I don't mind."

"There isn't enough room for the three of us in Jay's kitchen. The only times I'm allowed in there is when I'm cooking out on the grill, fixing coffee, or helping clean up. Go relax." Kenny urged her toward the other room.

When both men had finished dealing with the leftovers and dirty dishes, they joined her on the couch with one on either side of her. Rayna couldn't stop the little thrill that drag-raced down her spine at the closeness of both men. How was she going to be able to handle sitting through a movie like this?

I'm going to end up hurt over this. I can already tell.

"So, we have just about anything you might want to watch from comedy to shootouts to dramas. What are you in the mood for?" Jay asked her.

"Oh, well. I like just about anything except the really raunchy comedies. What do you suggest?" she asked.

"Hey, Jay. Let's watch *Godzilla*. The new one." Kenny stretched his long legs out as he rested one arm along the back of the couch behind her.

"That okay with you, Rayna?" Jay asked.

"Sure. I watched all of the old ones, but I haven't seen this one yet."

Jay set up the DVD player then returned to the couch, sitting a fair distance away from her. She began to relax some as the movie started. It wasn't until the next movie that they watched, some sort of comedy, that she found herself relaxing into both men as the good food, great wine, and congenial atmosphere caught up with her. The next thing she knew, Rayna woke up cocooned between both men so that she was warm and comfortable. Then it hit her where she was and what she was doing, and her eyes flew wide open.

Chapter Six

"Easy, babe. You're fine. The movie just went off. Hate that you missed it, but you must have been worn out. We can always watch it again next time." Kenny could tell Rayna was upset.

"I—I'm so sorry that I fell asleep on you guys. It must have been the wine. I don't usually do that."

"It's fine, Rayna. Really, it's fine." Jay stood up, extending his hand to her.

Kenny noticed how she hesitated and looked toward him before she accepted Jay's offer and let him pull her to her feet.

"I'm going to bed," Jay told them. "Rayna, it was great to get to know you. Hope you come back again, soon. I'll show you my shop."

"Thanks. I'd like that."

Kenny watched her face and noticed the unease when she told Jay she'd like to see his shop. Yep, she was attracted to both of them. Perfect. All he had to do was convince her to give them both a chance at the same time. He was positive her reaction wasn't going to be the one he wanted, but he'd change her mind. He had to. Kenny already felt the first stirrings of attachment to her. All three of them had, had a great time that night. Now it was up to him to make sure she didn't run screaming from the house.

"How are you feeling? Do you need to walk around a bit before you drive home?" Kenny asked.

"No. I think I'm wide-awake now. Thanks. I had a great evening, and the food and movies were excellent."

"I'm glad you did. What do you say we make plans to go hiking next Saturday if the weather permits? I'm usually finished at the clinic by noon. We could take a late picnic lunch and walk an easy trail to get you geared up for the harder ones later."

She smiled but started shaking her head. "I don't know, Kenny. I really like you, but I like Jay, as well. I didn't expect this to happen, but I can't date you or him since you're best friends. It wouldn't be fair to either of you or to me."

"It's okay, Rayna. We both like you, too. We want to date you together." Kenny waited as it slowly sank in and surprise swept across her face.

"Like a threesome? You want me to date both of you at the same time? I'm confused. Why would you want that?" she asked.

"Jay and I like to share. It's just what we like. We'd do everything in our power to make you happy. Just think, two men to wait on you hand and foot. Two men to make sure you're always happy, well fed, and well loved. There are a lot of threesomes in Riverbend. Since you don't get out much, I bet you haven't noticed them."

"There are other couples, I mean threesomes here? How many?" she asked. Her brows narrowed to meet over her nose.

"About six or seven families. Some have children. We can introduce you to some of them if you want."

"I don't know. I'm not sure I would be comfortable with dating two men at one time. Let me think about it, Kenny. I like you both a lot, but this is really different to how I was brought up."

Kenny sighed. "I understand, but at least agree to go hiking this weekend. You can get to know us better with no pressure. Just a short hike and lunch and that's all." He smiled, praying she'd agree.

"Maybe. I'll think about it and let you know later this week. Okay?" she asked.

I don't have a good feeling about this. She's balking. I've got to figure something out to get her to agree.

"I hope you really will think about it. It's not a big deal here in Riverbend. No one is going to judge you or say anything to you about it. It's just a way of life for some of us." He walked her to the door, making sure she had her sweater on before taking both of her shoulders in his hands. "Good night, Rayna."

He bent over her and gave her a light kiss that teased him as much as it would her then opened the door and turned on the outside light so she could see to get into her car. He walked her out but didn't attempt to kiss her again. She needed time. He got it. He didn't like it, but he understood. Kenny watched her back out of the drive then drive down the road to disappear into the dark. Then he sighed and walked back into the house.

"What did she say?" Jay asked when Kenny walked inside and locked the door.

"She'd think about it. She's spooked. I asked her to at least go hiking with us before she made up her mind, but I'm not sure she's going to go. She likes us both. She admitted that much."

Jay nodded. "That's a start, but I think she needs to talk to someone who's living the life that we want. Maybe we can get one of the other wives to go hiking with us. That would mean more people so not so tense for her. Plus, she can watch how they interact and maybe ask questions if we provide some time for her to do that."

"That's a great idea. I'll ask Jared and Quade if they and Lexie would go hiking with us. They would need to get a babysitter for their son, but I bet they'd enjoy getting out some by now." Kenny smiled. "I'll call them tomorrow and check in on their mare. She's about ready to foal."

"Good timing then. Kenny. I really like Rayna. She doesn't feel like any of the women we've dated in the past. She feels like home to me. Having her leaning on me while she slept earlier was the best I've felt in a long time." Jay leaned against the kitchen island. "What about you?"

"I feel the same way. She's special. She could be the one we've been waiting on all these years. Now all we have to do is convince her that she'd be happy with two men instead of just one."

* * * *

Rayna caught herself daydreaming between calls again. Ever since the night she'd eaten at Kenny and Jay's place, she'd been thinking about them at the oddest times. Her dreams had been sexy and embarrassing since she wasn't one to dream about two men at one time. Hell, she wasn't even one to dream about one man. She just didn't have such explicit dreams until she'd met Kenny and Jay. Now all of her thoughts were consumed by them.

Would it be so bad to date both of them at one time? Maybe. Maybe not. All she could think of was how much she'd enjoyed the night they'd eaten at their place. They'd both waited on her but hadn't pushed her for more than she was comfortable with. Neither man had tried to make out with her during the movie. In fact, she'd obviously been the one to end up curled up next to Jay. Kenny hadn't seemed to care that she'd done it either.

Rayna was no closer to making up her mind about hiking that weekend as when Kenny had asked her. Being out in the middle of nowhere with two men who wanted to date her sounded like a bad idea. But that was silly since Kenny was the town's veterinarian and wouldn't risk his reputation by pulling something with her out there. Still, did she want to encourage them if she wasn't going to date both of them?

It was already Thursday, and she needed to call Kenny to give him an answer instead of putting it off until the last minute. She sighed and decided to tell him that she couldn't do it. He'd understand and hopefully not pressure her. The instant she made the decision to turn them down, her chest started aching as if she'd lost her best friend.

I can't do it. It would be too hard to deal with two male egos at one time. What happens if I get mad at them? How could I ever win an argument when there are two against one?

Most of her thoughts were silly, but she'd made up her mind. She sighed and called the number Kenny had given her to use.

"Hello?"

"Hey, Kenny. It's Rayna."

"Hey, Rayna. I was actually about to call you. One of the threesomes I told you about is going to go hiking with us on Saturday. Do you know Jared, Quade, or Lexie? They just had their first son two months ago."

"I think I've met Lexie once at the diner. She was pregnant then, but I didn't know she was in a threesome with two men." Her resolve to say no shifted slightly.

"They're great friends. The men run a ranch, and she runs them." He chuckled.

"I bet the little boy runs all of them now." She laughed.

"You're probably right. So, are you game to meet them?"

"Well, I was going to say no, but since you've already asked them, I guess I'll go. I'm still not sure about all of this, Kenny. I'm afraid we're just putting off the inevitable."

"Just give us a chance, babe. I promise you'll have a great time, and Lexie will be more than happy to tell you what living with two men is like. We aren't asking you to marry us or anything. Just date us and see how things go."

"Okay. I'll keep an open mind and go hiking. Where and when?" she asked.

"I'll pick you up on the way home from the clinic at say twelve thirty. We'll pick up Jay and meet the others at one. Be sure and eat a little something and hydrate yourself before we go."

Rayna felt her mouth curve up into a wide grin. She was actually going to go, and she felt like she'd enjoy it with the other woman along to talk to.

"Okay. I'll see you Saturday."

Once again, she needed to find something to wear. She had some shorts that would be good for a short hike. They reached just above her knees. She wasn't sure if a regular T-shirt was best or a sleeveless top would be better. In the end, she opted to wear an overly large T-shirt over a sleeveless top in case she needed to remove the T-shirt if she got hot.

Rayna pondered how a threesome relationship actually worked. Did the woman spend time with both men all the time, or did they do things separately at times? Did they all three sleep in one bed, or did the woman sleep with a different man each night? How did it work out when they decided to have children? Did one of them agree to let the other one have the first kid, or was it just the luck of the draw?

She shook her head.

I've got too many questions. I'm going to have to wait and see what Lexie is comfortable talking about.

She couldn't believe she was actually going to go out with two men at one time. By going on the hike, she'd basically agreed to do just that. What had happened to telling them no? She swore she'd made up her mind to call and tell Kenny she couldn't handle it.

Rayna logged off her shift and updated her paperwork before going to check on Patches. The sweet momma was asleep in the box with her babies lined up at her belly sleeping, as well. She had one paw across two of the little kitties. They were all so cute it was going to be hard to let them go when it was time to find homes for them. Hopefully she could put a notice at Kenny's office and find good homes for them that way. She was sure anyone who visited the vet would provide a good environment for them. She'd ask him when he picked her up on Saturday.

I can't believe I'm really doing this. It's only a double, um, co-date? What did you call it when two sets of three did something together?

A party?

Chapter Seven

At twelve thirty, a knock at her door sent lunatic hummingbirds careening around inside of Rayna's stomach. She swore she was going to throw up if they didn't settle down.

When she opened the door, it was to find both Jay and Kenny standing outside her door in sexy shorts and tank tops. She was sure her mouth dropped open, but she made sure to close it.

"I got finished early so I went ahead and picked up Jay before coming to get you. I didn't want to catch you unprepared."

"That's fine. I'm ready. I have water and a first aid kit in my pack."

Jay spoke up. "No need for you to carry a pack this first time. We've got everything covered."

"I don't want to leave it all on you guys. I can help."

"We know, babe, but there's no need when we can carry it." Kenny took the pack from her hands and set it just inside the doorway.

"Oh, um, unless you have personal items you needed to carry." Jay's face reddened slightly, making Rayna laugh.

"No, nothing like that. I'm fine. I just feel like I'm putting all the work on you guys." She smiled.

"That's what we're for," Kenny told her. "To do all the work. Let's go and meet up with the others."

Rayna locked her door then walked ahead of the two men to the truck. Kenny drove, so it was Jay who helped her up into the front seat. He climbed in next to her, sandwiching her between the two men. At first she tried to keep from touching either of them but realized all she was doing was tiring out herself, so she relaxed and didn't worry if she touched either man.

If I'm going to have an open mind about dating two men, I need to stop obsessing about who I do and don't touch or talk to.

That wasn't as easy as she thought it should be. She found herself keeping score on who she talked to last and which one she'd asked the last question of. She was going to be exhausted by the time they reached the trailhead where they were going to be hiking.

Once they arrived, Jay leaned over and whispered, "I can tell you're nervous about all of this, Rayna. Don't be. Just relax and have a good time. There's no rules to this. If you don't enjoy yourself, then what's the fun in going?"

She couldn't stop the smile that filled her face. Jay was right. It was all about having fun and visiting with each other. It wasn't a competition or a test.

"There they are now," Kenny said.

Three people piled out of a truck equally as large as Kenny's was. The two men towered over the pretty woman. It was obvious that the men doted on her by the way they each held one of her hands and kissed the top of her head as they walked closer.

"Hey, Kenny, Jay. How's it going?" one man asked.

"Good, good. Guys, this is Rayna. Rayna, this is Lexie and her husbands, Jared and Quade." Kenny pointed each of them out as he made the introductions.

"It's great to meet you guys. Thanks for coming along." She wasn't sure what more to say. She couldn't say and "thanks for letting me watch how you guys interact because I'm worried about dating two men at once."

"This will be fun. We've gone on a few of the trails closer to the house, but this one is really nice they tell me." Lexie donned a small pack with the help of Quade. The two men pulled on much larger packs. Rayna didn't feel quite as useless as she had earlier.

"Let's get going. I want to get to the waterfall before it gets too late so we can enjoy it," Jay said.

"Oh, I forgot about that. I can't wait." Lexie positioned herself next to Rayna as they started off. Two guys in front and two behind them.

Kenny pointed out various flowers and a flustered rabbit as they walked. Rayna found herself having a wonderful time. Still, she wanted to talk to Lexie without the guys so close by. Maybe when they stopped for a water break she could ask her then.

At the first break, Jay handed her a bottle of water and a nut bar. He returned to talk with the other guys, and she and Lexie settled on a flat rock to talk.

"So, what do you think of Jay and Kenny?" Lexie asked.

"I like them. I mean they're really nice."

"Are you nervous about dating two guys? I can understand that. It feels weird to have two men always around and all."

"Were you uncomfortable with dating them both?" she asked.

"I guess I didn't have that worry. They rescued me from a bad relationship that was abusive. I never really worried about there being two of them. I can see how it would bother you though."

Rayna sighed. "Don't you feel weird with walking in town so that everyone sees you?"

"No, I really don't. There are four or five families around here, plus there are some other alternative lifestyles in Riverbend." Lexie sipped on her water.

"Alternative lifestyles? What's that?"

"Well, we have an alternative lifestyle, and there are others who are in a D/s relationship. That means Dominant/submissive relationship. Have you heard of that?"

"Like *Fifty Shades*?" Rayna asked.

"That's right for the most part. It's complicated, and *Fifty Shades* didn't adequately cover it." Lexie recapped her empty bottle. "The thing is it's a wonderful life. I haven't regretted it one second, and now I have a beautiful son with my husbands."

"Don't you ever fight or have disagreements?"

"Oh, honey, there will be the normal fusses and arguments, but the nice thing is that you get to make up afterward. It's no different than any other relationship. You work through the tough times and enjoy the good times."

"Do you do everything as a group, or do you alternate?"

"It all depends. Sometimes we're all together like out at dinner or shopping, but sometimes one of them has something they've got to do and it's just two of us. I don't keep score if that's what you're referring to. The only time I don't get my way is if it involves something that would be dangerous or if my health is in question." Lexie smiled. "There were a lot of fireworks while I was pregnant. My poor obstetrician earned his payment. I was calling him every week it seemed to get him to tell the guys that it was safe for me to swim or do things around the house."

Rayna chuckled. "I can imagine those conversations. So what are the downfalls? There have to be some."

Lexie cocked her head to one side. "Honestly, I can't think of any other than there are two men saying no when they think you're about to do something that's detrimental to your health. Otherwise, it's great. There's always someone around to get something off a tall shelf for you. I guess the one downside is that sometimes I want a little me time. I usually get that by telling them I want to take a bubble bath alone. Then they make sure I have everything I need and leave me alone. Mostly."

"Mostly?"

"Yeah, they check every fifteen or so minutes to be sure I haven't fallen asleep and drowned."

Rayna laughed. "I can imagine that would get to be annoying, as well."

"You learn to deal with it."

"You guys ready to go?" Jared called over.

"Yeah." Rayna stood up and recapped her empty bottle. They gave the empties and the wrappers to Quade, who tucked them into his backpack.

"How much farther to the waterfall?" Rayna asked Kenny.

"About thirty minutes. Won't be long now."

Rayna and Lexie kept up a soft conversation about everyday things. Rayna kept thinking over what the other woman had told her. It sounded like she was very happy, and the way the guys seemed to dote on her, Rayna could see why. Would it be the same way with Jay and Kenny?

Soon the sound of a loud roaring could be heard as they neared the falls. Lexie expected a huge drop but was surprised when they squeezed through several rocks to find a mere ten-foot drop. Kenny explained that the enclosed rocks echoed, making the falls seem much larger than they were.

"It's too cold to swim in now, but soon we can come back and actually swim in the pool. You can soak your feet if you want to," Kenny said.

"I'm all for getting my feet wet," Lexie said.

"Are you sure, baby? I don't want you to catch a cold." Quade helped her sit down next to the water.

Lexie made a face and turned to Rayna. "See what I mean."

Rayna laughed. "I see." She started removing her shoes but had her hands brushed aside as Jay took over unlacing her shoes and pulling them and her socks off. She noticed that Quade was doing the same for Lexie.

They dipped their feet into the cool water and giggled at how silly they felt pulling them right back out, only to drop them back down. She and Lexie chatted about mundane things for the next thirty minutes. It wasn't long before the guys urged them to take their feet out and let them dry so they could pull their socks and shoes back on to head back down the little trail.

The trip back down was made in a companionable silence with only a few quick sentences when Kenny spotted something he thought the women would enjoy. A couple of deer stood off the trail munching away on sprigs of grass. They'd remained there for another few minutes until the animals had wandered away.

Rayna could easily say it had been one of the best days of her life. How could she possibly throw away more days like that by refusing to date Kenny and Jay at the same time? If nothing came of their dates, she would be able to say she'd tried. If she refused to see them both, she'd never know if there could have been more that she'd missed by being a prude.

"What are you thinking about so hard?" Kenny asked as he helped her up into the front seat of the truck.

"Just thinking. I had a great time today. Thank you both for having me."

Jay climbed up behind the wheel this time. "It was all our pleasure. I'm thankful that you agreed to give it a go. Was Lexie able to answer all of your questions?"

"Pretty much. I think some of them are only really up to me and what I'm comfortable with. They sure are a great family. I can't get over how attentive the men are over her."

"They love her. They'd do anything to make her smile," Jay told her.

"I'm not sure I could handle all of that togetherness all the time though. I'm used to being alone all the time. I would think a relationship like that would smother me."

"Bethany Tidwell is like that. She is a writer, and her two husbands understand that she needs quiet time without them hovering. With their jobs, they aren't always watching over her. Mac is the sheriff, and his brother is an attorney." Kenny squeezed her hand. "Every relationship is different, despite all of them being threesomes. It's what you make them."

"How do we know how to go about making our own? I mean we hardly know each other. It's bound to take time to forge a strong relationship when there are three of us."

Jay nodded. "It takes time, but all good, solid relationships take time to create and maintain. You don't start one and then just exist in it. You have to work on them all the time."

"I can see that." Rayna shifted in the seat. "I'm leaning toward giving the three of us a try, but I want to sleep on it. Is that okay?"

Jay nodded. "We're good with that. Just don't say no."

Rayna chuckled. "No pressure, huh?"

"Never."

Chapter Eight

Monday morning Rayna woke early from a restless night of dreams centered around Kenny and Jay. She'd never dreamed so much in one night before. They'd dated, gotten married, and had three kids, two dogs, and a half-dozen cats. All of it frightened her as much as she'd enjoyed the dream. Six cats? What would they do with six of them?

She checked on Patches and found that the mother cat had stretched out between the box holding her kittens and the fireplace once again. She looked so satisfied and was slowly adding more hair and a little bit of meat to her bones. She'd been the perfect pet so far. All Rayna had to do was keep her food bowl full, her water bowl clean, and empty the litter box. She got purrs and soft pats on her face when the cat jumped up on her lap while she was reading.

Would dating both Jay and Kenny at the same time go as smoothly? Was she actually considering it?

Yes. She was.

They'd been perfect gentlemen, fun companions, and were different enough that she had no trouble seeing herself spending time both together and separately with one or the other. Kenny would be busy with his veterinarian practice and Jay with his woodworking. She could continue her job without feeling like she was ignoring them and feeling guilty about it. They could date weekends and talk during the week at night.

Rayna could see where it could work. She could also see herself worrying over if she'd offended one with spending too much time with the other. That worried her. She'd always been one to play fair.

If she had to worry about that, it would never work. She would worry herself sick.

Lexie had said they didn't worry about that. Sometimes she spent more time with one man when the other one was busy, but it all worked out in the end. She'd told her that jealousy never figured into their relationship.

Could it really be that easy? She started when her cell rang, jerking her out of her thoughts. She picked up the phone but didn't recognize the number.

"Hello?"

"Hey, Rayna, it's Lexie. I hope you don't mind that I got your number from the guys. I wanted to call and thank you for asking us on your hike. I had a blast. It was the first real outing we'd had since the babe came."

"It's fine. I'm so glad you enjoyed yourself, but I'm the one who's thankful for your coming along. You answered so many of the questions circling in my head and driving me crazy." Rayna curled up in her favorite chair with her feet under her.

"I bet you still have some questions. The guys are out at the barn looking over a horse they're planning to sell. We're all alone, so ask whatever you want to. I don't mind answering." Lexie's sweet voice held an edge of naughty to it.

"Do you all sleep together, or do you sleep in a different man's bed each night?" Rayna popped her hand over her mouth. "I'm sorry. That was too personal."

"Not at all. I told you we were all alone and could talk about anything," she said with what Rayna was sure was a smile on her face. "We sleep all together. Sometimes it's just me and one of the guys if the other one is out all night with a foaling or something going on with the cattle, but that doesn't happen very often. Oh, and I don't have sex every single night. At least not anymore. That gets tiring, and after a while, you end up too sore to walk."

"I would imagine so." Rayna fanned her face. "Don't they ever get jealous of each other?"

"Nope. If they did, they never let me know about it. We all spend quality time together and apart. Out of all of the threesome couples, or triads, as some call them, ours is probably the only one with my men close to me all the time since we all live and work on the ranch. The others have outside jobs for the most part."

"You seem so happy. I guess I worry that there would be too much tension to make it work."

Lexie chuckled. "The only tension in a threesome that isn't centered around sex is what you make yourself go through. My advice is to relax and see where it takes you. You might see in a few weeks or months that it just isn't for you, but you tried and wouldn't always be second-guessing if you'd made the right decision or not. For all you know, it just might work out."

"Maybe you're right. I can't help but be nervous though. I haven't dated much at all in the last few years. So, jumping into this seems pretty major to me."

"I understand. Just know that anytime you have questions, call me. I'll be glad to talk. Hell, if you just want to talk or have a cup of coffee, come over and visit. I do a lot of the office work here, but I'm not on any schedule. I'd love to be friends."

"Thank you, Lexie. I'd like that. I really don't know many people here, and I've lived here for a long time. When I first fell in love with the town after searching for somewhere quiet and laid back, I never dreamed I wouldn't get out more and meet people."

Rayna ended the call and added Lexie to her contacts. She scrolled through her very few saved contacts and realized she didn't have Jay's number, only Kenny's number. She decided to call Kenny and request Jay's number from him. How he reacted would determine if she could see dating them both.

She selected his number and waited as it rang. It went to voice mail, so she determined he was busy with a patient. She left her name and number then ended the call.

Twenty minutes later, her phone rang. She saw that it was Kenny and answered.

"Hi. Sorry to bother you at work," she said.

"It's no bother. What can I do for you?"

"I don't have Jay's number. Could I get it from you?"

"Sure. Do you have a pen ready?"

"Go."

He rattled off the number while she wrote it down.

"If you call him, let him know I'm going to be late tonight. I have a couple of teeth cleanings I've had to put off until later due to a couple of emergencies. He gets grouchy if I don't let him know when he's cooked something."

"I'll let him know. Thanks for the number."

"Bye, babe."

He hadn't seemed the least bit jealous that she'd asked for Jay's number. Maybe things would work out if she just gave it a chance. Rayna called Jay next. He answered on the fourth ring just before she was about to hang up."

"This is Jay. How can I help you?"

"Um, hi, Jay. This is Rayna. I didn't realize this was your business number. I'm sorry."

"No problem. It's my only number. Kenny must have given it to you. I forgot all about giving it to you the other day when we went hiking."

"I wanted to add it to my contacts listing. I had his but not yours."

There was a silence on the other end for a split second, and then he laughed. "That's great. You're going to give this a chance, right?"

"Yeah. I am. I really enjoyed myself the other day, and I know I'd kick myself if I said no without finding out if we could have a good time together."

"This is great news. So, do you mind if I tell Kenny, or have you already said something to him?"

"No. You can. Oh, and he was busy, something about he's going to be late tonight due to cleaning teeth. Do animals go to dentists?" she asked.

Jay's smile was evident in his voice. "Actually, in a way, yes. Dogs and cats need teeth cleanings to keep from getting gum disease and losing teeth. Plus, if you don't do it regularly, it can lead to kidney disease."

"You should be a veterinarian spokesperson." Rayna laughed.

"I've heard it so many times now that I could probably do the job. Don't get me started on heartworm medication."

"Oh my God. I'm going to break a rib laughing. Thanks. I needed this."

"Since Kenny is going to be late for dinner, why don't you come over and we can eat it when it's ready and he can have leftovers?

"Oh. Um. I don't want to leave him without something to eat."

"Honey, if you eat all of what I have cooked, I'll cook him another meal. I have enough for three or four days. That's what I do. Cook big batches and we eat leftovers when he's busy or I'm too busy to cook anything. I just finished a job, so I was cooking up before I end up busy again."

"Okay. I'd like that. What time?" she asked.

"Just whenever you want to come over."

"I have another hour of calls and paperwork. How about five?"

"See you then, sweetheart."

* * * *

Jay had Rayna doubled over laughing when Kenny walked in at just shy of seven that night. Her laughing eyes and the broad smile across her face warmed his soul.

"Hey there. What a wonderful sound to come home to. Is he tickling you or telling tales?" he asked as he hung up his jacket next to the door.

"I just found out that you got in trouble for bringing home wild animals to doctor on when you were eight." She giggled.

"I see. Maybe I should tell about the time you caught your mom's kitchen on fire trying to make that flaming dessert you'd seen on TV."

"Too late, I told her that one because I knew you would eventually." Jay laughed as he started heating up Kenny's meal in the microwave.

"You guys going to keep me company while I eat?" Kenny asked.

"I will for a few minutes, and then I've got to go home. I work early shift so I have to be up by five to be ready and coherent."

"I understand that. Did Jay show you his shop? It's kind of amazing if you're not scared you'll cut your hand off or something."

Rayna smiled at him then looked across at Jay. "He did. He even let me turn the lathe on a chair leg. It was fun."

"Hey! I had to beg to get you to let me cut out one of my own bookshelves." Kenny scowled at his friend.

"You didn't smile pretty for me." Jay winked at Rayna.

Everything seemed to be going great. He had no doubt this had been a test to see if he got jealous because she'd asked for Jay's number and then had come over to spend time with him without Kenny being there. She'd learn that they didn't get jealous as long as the three of them were connected.

"Here you go. We have enough for another meal for maybe Wednesday or Thursday. I'll make sandwiches tomorrow night."

"Sounds good." Kenny sat down and started eating. "How was your day, babe?"

"About normal. I did have a funny call about a drug. The lady was questioning some of her husband's medication payments and wasn't sure why one of them wasn't covered on their supplementary card. I had to explain that their policy didn't cover erectile dysfunction medication. She got really quiet then asked me to repeat what I'd just said. She politely thanked me and screamed her husband's name before she hung up. I think he had a lot of explaining to do when she got hold of him."

Kenny and Jay both burst out laughing. Kenny nearly sprayed the iced tea across the bar before he swallowed it.

"That's funny," Kenny said. "Do you get very many calls like that?"

"Not really. A lot of my calls are bad news calls. Your policy doesn't cover this or yes, that is how much your deductible is. I hate those calls. I feel like I'm always giving bad news."

"I guess it would feel like that. Have you thought of doing something else?"

"Actually, I've been thinking about finishing my coding certificate and taking the exam so I could code insurance from home instead. I just haven't convinced myself that I can make as much money doing that as I do answering calls."

"I can tell you that you do much better if you like what you do in your job. Eventually you'll get burned out with one you don't really like, and then you could be stuck without a way out. I'd at least get your certificate on the coding thing and then decide." Jay reached out and squeezed her hand.

"Jay's right, babe. If you decide not to switch, you still have the certificate if you decide later you want to try it." Kenny took another bite from his plate and watched her.

"I'll think about it. It wouldn't take much more for me to be qualified to apply. I'll look it up and see where I stand with credits." She looked at the clock over the stove. "I better go. Thanks for dinner, Jay. Hope you both have a good night."

"I'll walk you to your car." Jay followed her to the door and opened it for her.

"Bye, babe. I'll talk to you later." Kenny lifted his iced tea glass as she smiled.

Once they'd walked out the door and Jay had closed it behind them, Kenny jumped up and walked over to listen to their conversation. It wasn't that he was jealous or wanted to snoop. He really just wanted to know if she was going to date them both. Her being here told him yes, but he wanted to know for sure. He really liked Rayna.

"I really enjoyed the tour of your shop, Jay, and you know dinner was amazing. I'm stuffed. I can't eat with you very often, or I'll be as big as a barn," she told him.

"Nonsense. You look amazing, and a few extra pounds wouldn't hurt you one bit. Thanks for coming over and keeping me company. I appreciate it."

Kenny watched as Jay held her door open then swept in and kissed her, his hand cupping her cheek as he did. Kenny smiled at the gentle way he was kissing her. Jay didn't normally do easy. He was usually more aggressive.

When Jay released her, Rayna slowly opened her eyes as a wide smile spread over her face. Kenny grinned.

Yes!

"Good night, Jay.

"Night, sweetheart."

Kenny couldn't wait until their next date. He'd talk to Jay about it as soon as he walked back in. They were in. She was going to date them both.

Chapter Nine

Rayna found herself shopping with Lexie Saturday morning to find something to wear Saturday night out with the guys. She'd talked to both of them off and on over the last week and had thoroughly enjoyed every conversation. This would be the first real out-of-her-comfort-zone date they'd had. They were going out to eat at the steakhouse just outside of town then dancing at the bar later that night.

"What about this? It's tasteful but has just a bit of sass to it, as well." Lexie held up a lovely Easter-grass-green dress with a low, scooped neck and an A-line form.

"I love it. I'll try it on." She took the dress and located the sales clerk to open the dressing room door for her.

Once she had it on, she twirled to look in the glass and was pleased that it hid her slightly large hips. She opened the door to let Lexie see.

"Oh, that is perfect. You have to get that one," the other woman said.

"You like it?"

"I love it. It brings out the green in your eyes. You have pretty eyes, Rayna."

"Thanks. I'll get dressed. I think we've just about got it nailed down."

"Shoes are next," Lexie called out over the door.

"I hear you."

Rayna had never had so much fun shopping. At least not after her mother had died. They found some strappy green sandals with enough cushion for dancing that would go great with the dress. Then they shopped for a new pair of shoes for Lexie and a couple of outfits for her growing boy.

"I swear he's going to be taller than his fathers if he keeps growing. This is the second time in two weeks that I've had to get larger pants because his legs stick out too far." Lexie squeezed Rayna's shoulders. "Thank you so much for asking me to go shopping with you. I haven't been out without little Marcus since we went hiking."

"Don't worry about it. I needed help, and you're the only other person I know to have asked for this kind of help. Normally I'm asking for the name of a good plumber or an electrician."

"Those days are behind you. No matter what comes of your relationship with Kenny and Jay, we're still friends. Got it?" Lexie asked.

"Got it. Thanks."

"So are the fireworks there?"

"Oh, um. Yeah, I guess you could say that. We've only really kissed a little. I think they're going slow for me." Rayna was sure they were since she'd noticed how hard a certain part of their anatomy had been the few times they'd been together.

"That's good. They're serious about you then. They aren't just in it for a bed partner. They're looking for a romance, someone to come home to every day. That's super!"

"Really? You think so?"

"Yep. Men around here either go hard and heavy when they aren't looking for more than sex, or they go achingly slow and drive you crazy while you wait for the big punch. It can drive you insane while you wait for them to do something interesting." Lexie smiled. "If you want things to heat up a little faster, tease them so that they can't handle the stress and make a move. It won't change how they feel about you one bit other than maybe speed up the process of the bed-partner part."

"Goodness. I'm not sure if I can tease them. I haven't really gone out on many dates. I mean maybe a few dozen in the last eight or ten years."

"Here's what you do," Lexie began, helping her create a plan of attack.

They had a light lunch at the diner and talked about the town and some of the local gossip. Then they split up so that Rayna could go home to get ready for her date.

She carefully hung the dress up and set the box of new shoes on the floor beneath it. She hadn't had that much fun in a long time. If nothing happened between them, she would never regret one minute of her dating the two guys. They'd opened up her world to others and gotten her out of her little house.

She took a quick shower then ran water in the tub to shave her legs and trim her toenails before drying them and adding the same color as her fingernails to her toes. She rubbed in her favorite lightly scented lotion and looked at herself in the bathroom's full mirror. Her hips were a little larger than she liked and her stomach rounder and softer than she'd have wished, but she felt like she looked pretty good for a stay-at-home worker. She needed to get out and exercise more. Maybe hiking would become her new hobby. She'd enjoyed it and had definitely felt the effects the next day.

If things work out with the guys, we can hike at least once a month when it isn't bad weather.

Deep down inside, she prayed that it would work out. She already liked both of them a little more than she'd believed she would so soon. They seemed to make everything about her and didn't resent it.

I could easily fall in love with them. Both of them, though? Maybe. I'm not sure how that works.

Once she had her dress and shoes on, Rayna spent a little more time with her hair and makeup. She didn't like to wear a lot of stuff on her face, but a little eyeshadow and mascara along with a swipe of lip-gloss wouldn't be too much. She slipped the lip-gloss into her hip purse and added a powder pack to dab her forehead and cheeks if she got sweaty dancing.

Crap! How did that work? Did all three of them dance together, or would they each take turns on the floor with her? She was going to need to start an exercise program just to keep up with them if she had to dance with both of them all night.

When the doorbell rang, Rayna nearly screamed in surprise. She checked the time and realized she'd been daydreaming away her time. She opened the door to find Kenny standing just outside with a long-stem red rose.

"A rose for a rose." He handed it to her.

"That is so sweet. Let me put it in water so it won't die. Come in. Is Jay out in the truck?"

"Yep. He's driving. I'm gathering our woman up to take her out to eat."

Rayna found a bud vase, and after cutting off an inch of the stem, set it in the vase and left it on the kitchen counter.

"Do you think Patches will bother it?" she asked.

"I doubt it. How is the little momma doing?" he asked.

"Look for yourself." She pointed to Patches curled up on the cushion on the floor next to the box of kittens.

Kenny looked inside the box then gave Patches a quick rub. "Good momma. You're doing really well there."

"She is. I've never had a pet before, but I don't do anything for her except food, water, and litter tray. When she wants affection, she jumps up in my lap while I'm talking on the phone, and I pet her while I talk."

"That's a perfect pet. Will you keep her and the kittens or find them homes?" he asked as he closed the door for her.

"I'm keeping Patches and finding homes for at least three of the kittens. I figured I might keep one of the kittens to keep her company." She locked the door then dropped her key into her bag.

"That's a good idea. We can post them on our board when they're old enough."

"That's what I was hoping for."

He helped her climb up into the truck then sat next to her.

"Hi, Jay. How are you doing?" she asked.

"Great now that you're sitting next to me. I was about to come in and rescue you."

"Sorry, I had to show off Patches and the kittens to Kenny. They're growing so fast."

"That's fine. I was just kidding." He squeezed her hand.

"Thank you for the rose. I figured it was from both of you?" she asked, a little unsure.

"Yep. We decided two roses looked kind of odd in a vase. We decided one from both of us would be fine." Jay started the truck.

"You thought perfectly. Hey, when the kittens are ready, do you want a shop cat?"

Kenny burst out laughing.

Rayna frowned. "What?"

"I just won a bet," Kenny told her.

"A bet? You bet on me?" she asked.

"Yeah, I bet Jay that you'd ask him if he wanted a cat before they were six weeks old. He bet you wouldn't ask until you'd put them up for adoption."

"What if I hadn't asked at all?" She scowled at them.

"Then it was a draw, but really, Rayna. You'd have asked eventually."

She sighed and smiled. "Yeah. I would. The best home for a rescued animal is with a vet or at the home of a vet."

"So, I win. You can pay up next weekend, bro."

"What does he win?" she asked Jay.

"I have to wash his truck, as well as mine," he said.

"So, do you want a shop kitty?"

* * * *

Rayna was positive the date was going perfectly. They'd had a great dinner where she hadn't felt too nervous about being out with the two of them. Now they were at the bar and had found Brody, Lamar, and Caitlyn there, as well. Caitlyn was expecting and just beginning to show. They all six shared a table and were having a wonderful time.

"So when Lamar asked the man what the cage was for, he told him it was for his wife. She liked him to tie her up sometimes, and the cage was going to be for her birthday." Caitlyn chuckled.

"Oh. My. God. Really? People do that?"

"Yep. They've gotten some odd requests, but that is the wildest so far." Caitlyn sipped at her ginger ale. "How are things going with you and the guys? They can't seem to take their eyes off of you."

"Really? I think we're doing pretty good. I wasn't too sure about a threesome kind of relationship, but I talked with Lexie, and now talking to you, I'm seeing that it might be the perfect kind." Rayna looked over to see that Jay was watching her with a soft smile. Seconds later, Kenny looked her direction.

"See what I mean? There are ups and downs just like in any marriage, but to me, the pros far outweigh the cons."

"I'm beginning to see that. It hasn't been but a couple of weeks, so I'm still learning how it all works. I really like being with them and enjoy their different personalities," she told the other woman.

"The new stage is the fun stage. Everything is so fresh, and you're just getting your feet wet. Later, you get comfortable with them, and you aren't as cautious about things you say or do. You'll see."

"I guess I'm still a little nervous about it, but I'm not running."

"Good. Just give them a few weeks and you'll be wondering why anyone would want to stick to just one man." She winked at Rayna. "You'll see what I mean."

She could feel her cheeks heating up at the innuendo behind the wink she'd given her.

"Hey, babe. Let's dance." Kenny stood over her, holding out his hand.

"I'd love to." She accepted his hand and stood up.

He led her to the crowded dance floor and pulled her into his arms where they swayed to the gentle beat of "Unchained Melody."

"Thank you for saving me. I was getting embarrassed."

"I noticed your face getting that sweet shade of pink that looks so good on you." He pulled her closer so that she could feel the long line of his hard dick against her belly. "What was Caitlyn telling you about?"

"Nothing really. She just gave some little hints, and my imagination got away from me."

"Oh really? Like what was one of the hints?" Kenny asked.

"Not on your life. I'm not going there." She giggled and rubbed her pelvis lightly against the bulge snaking its way down his leg.

"Two can play at that game, babe." He turned her slightly so that when he moved her back against him her nipples raked across the buttons on his shirt.

"Oh my." She felt her entire body begin to burn.

"See." He grinned down at her. "But feel free to continue doing it. I'm really not complaining."

She laughed with him.

"If we haven't already said it, you look amazing in that dress. It really complements your hair and your green eyes."

She knew her face was moving from pleasantly pink to fire-engine red now.

The song ended, and another faster one took its place. "Ready to call it a night?"

"Yeah. I think that's a good idea," she said.

They returned to the table, and Kenny made their excuses. "We've worn our date out. I think she's ready to go."

"I had a great time, you guys. Maybe we can do it again."

"I'll call you, and me, you, and Lexie can go for a girl's day out one day," Caitlyn called out.

"Sounds great." She waved as Kenny pulled her along behind him. Jay followed up and made sure she didn't get stuck in the crowd.

Once they'd settled in the truck, Kenny asked her something she hadn't expected.

"Would you like to go home, or do you want to come back to our place with us?"

Chapter Ten

Jay waited to hear what Rayna would say. He knew what he wanted her to say but knew it might be too early for her to feel comfortable with getting serious.

"I'd like to go home with you two."

He squeezed the steering wheel so tight it was a wonder it didn't dent.

Yes!

"Sounds good," Kenny said.

If Jay hadn't known his friend any better he'd have thought he was fine with her choice, but he knew that Kenny was probably having to bite his tongue to keep from yelling in triumph. He'd been surprised when he'd even asked her so soon. That was usually him pushing at the more intimate step, not Kenny.

"Um, we didn't put up the hounds from hell," Jay reminded him.

"They'll be fine. I can put them up if they make a nuisance of themselves."

"Hounds from hell?" she asked.

Jay chuckled. "That's what I call them. We've got an English mastiff, a Great Dane. Then there are the cats. They just go about their business as if the other two aren't around."

"Wow. Those are large dogs. I didn't see them the other night when I ate with you guys."

"I'd put them up while you were there. I didn't want you to have to deal with them when you were still kind of new around us. They're great dogs. No biting tendencies at all."

"I'd love to meet them. Just don't leave me alone yet. I've never been around large dogs before."

"Don't worry. We won't." Kenny squeezed her hand then leaned over and kissed her.

Jay was jealous but only that he couldn't be a part of the kiss. He knew Kenny would be getting a good taste of their woman, but he'd get his own taste once they made it back to their place. He concentrated on taking it slow and driving safe so that they could see where Kenny's kiss took them.

Once he'd parked the truck, Jay jumped down and hurried around the front of the truck to unlock the house and act as a barrier for Rayna against the dogs. Depending on how she reacted to them, he would usher them to the back of the house where they could stay if needed.

Kenny helped their woman out of the truck then strolled to the door holding her hand. When they stepped inside, the dogs went crazy at the scent of a new friend.

"Down, boys and girls. There's no need to scare our guest to death," he told them.

"Rayna, this is Chester, the English mastiff. This is Roxie, the Great Dane, and I'll introduce the cats when they decide to grace us with their presence. He's got some sort of bulldog in him with those jowls and that big head, so we thought the name fit." Kenny made the introductions where he held her hand in his out to each of the dogs. They whined and licked and slobbered like all good dogs tended to do.

"What about the cat? You said you had a cat, as well."

"She's around here somewhere. If she shows herself we'll introduce you to her. Her name is Gidget," Jay told her.

"Let's get you out of that sweater. Would you like something to drink? We've got wine if you'd like a glass," Kenny said.

"No, I've had plenty to drink for one night. I'll take some iced tea or lemonade, whichever you have fixed."

"I'll get it. We've got both, but I'll fix lemonade." Jay walked into the kitchen while his friend hung up Rayna's sweater and urged her to sit on the couch.

Kenny walked over and turned on some music before returning to sit next to her. Jay returned with three glasses of lemonade and sat on the other side of her. He handed Kenny his then clinked glasses with both of them.

"To us and getting to know each other better."

"I agree,' Kenny said.

"To getting to know each other," Rayna said.

They sipped the lemonade, and then a song came on that she obviously liked. Jay stood up after taking her glass and setting it on the coffee table. "Let's dance."

She stood up and followed him around the table and let him take her into his arms. When she was relaxed and swaying with him to the soft beat, Kenny stood up and caged her in from behind. He wasn't shoving her into Jay, just gently moving with her at first. Then he leaned in and lifted her hair to one side so that he had access to her neck. Jay watched Rayna's expression when his friend licked her neck down to the area where her dress began then back up again. Her eyes closed, and her mouth opened just a tiny bit.

He nodded at Kenny to continue. His friend nibbled her neck and up along her jawline before spreading kisses back down her neck. Jay kissed Rayna's mouth, licking along the seam of her lips to gain entrance, and then he swept inside to explore every part of her. She tasted of lemonade and something sweet. He could kiss her all night. But he slowly pulled back and kissed his way to the corner of her mouth and then over to her ear lobe, where he sucked on it, and moved back to end at her mouth once more. When he pulled back, her eyes were closed and her head leaned to one side.

Awesome.

"Rayna, as much as we like making out with you on the couch, we're a little old for it. Can we take you to our bedroom?" Jay asked.

"Bedroom?" Her eyes opened but were still heavy-lidded. "I'd like that."

Kenny picked her up and carried her around the other side of the kitchen where the master suite, which they'd never used, was located. He'd freshened it up in case they got this chance, but they both kept rooms upstairs. This was for when they eventually married and shared it with the woman of their dreams. Jay was hoping that would turn out to be Rayna.

"Put me down, Kenny. You'll hurt yourself." Rayna's outraged voice only made Jay laugh.

"Believe me, sweetness. He can carry just fine. You don't weigh near as much as you think you do." Joe reached over and squeezed her hand as it held on to the back of Kenny's neck.

"Oh. This is pretty. Whose room is this?" Rayna looked from the spacious bed over to the three doors lining one of the walls.

Neither of us uses this room right now.

"There are two walk-in closets, and the middle door opens into the bathroom," Kenny pointed out.

"I love the colors. They're so warm."

Jay didn't know about how warm they were, but he liked the rust and orange colors. The hardwood floors looked great with them and the built-ins he'd added worked well with both colors.

Kenny eased Rayna to the floor before pulling her into a kiss, holding her cheeks in his hands. Jay waited his turn then turned her into his arms where he once again explored her mouth. It was just as amazing as it had been before, only better, as he was able to run his hands up and down her back.

Kenny unzipped her dress and slowly lowered it from behind. When she stepped out of it without breaking their kiss, Jay's dick hardened even more. His balls were already tight enough to squeeze lemons with. He didn't think he'd last long if they did much more messing around.

Evidently Kenny thought the same thing. He unfastened Rayna's bra, and after removing it, began undressing himself. Jay ran his hand over her breast, pausing to flick the already hardened nipple with his thumbnail. She moaned into his mouth as he rubbed the little nub. That sound went straight to his cock, causing him to groan back into her mouth.

Kenny turned her toward him now. He picked her up again and laid her back on the bed before he removed her sandals then went for her panties. Jay watched as he undressed how Rayna's eyes changed expressions. They went from dreamy soft to amazed when she caught sight of Kenny's cock then his own. They were big men, but not alarmingly so. He knew she was impressed when she licked her bottom lip as if wanting to taste them. He was all for that, but she came first.

"Easy, sweetheart. Let us take care of you. Just relax," he told her as he crawled up one side of the bed while Kenny took the other side.

"God, you're both so big. I'm not sure this will work."

"Are you trying to stroke my ego or what?" Kenny joked.

They both latched onto a nipple apiece and began sucking so that anything else she might have said was forgotten. They licked and sucked and nipped all around her breasts then up and down her neck. It didn't take long before she was digging her nails into their scalps begging them for something. Jay knew exactly what she needed. He inched lower and trailed a line of kisses down her chest to her abdomen, where he spent some time licking around her belly button then down to the little juncture where her thigh met her pelvis. She cried out as she bucked under them.

"Note to self. Makes her scream at this spot." Jay grinned when she scowled at him.

He spread her legs so that he could fit his shoulders between them and have access to her sweet pussy. He could already smell how aroused she'd become. The heady aroma went straight to his cock, making it difficult to lie still on the bed. He wanted to rub his dick against the rough spread, but didn't. Instead, he spread Rayna's pussy lips and licked from the bottom of her slit to the top, where he teased the little clit before sucking one of the fat little labia into his mouth to torment. He changed sides and laughed around it when he had to put one hand on her pelvis to keep her still.

She was a wildcat. He'd known she would be just by how she'd responded to their playing around while they'd danced that night. He couldn't wait to sink his dick deep into her pussy. Tonight, he'd get her mouth while Kenny took her cunt, but they'd have all night to explore her sexual needs. He wanted it to be amazing for her.

He lapped at her slit then slid one finger inside of her tight twat before adding a second one and pumping them in tandem with how he licked at her little clit. When he opened his eyes to look up to see how she was doing, it was to find her thrashing her head from side to side while his friend toyed with her tits using his lips and fingers.

She was ready to come. He could tell by how she thrashed and the way her pelvis jerked beneath his hand. He pumped his fingers in and out then sucked on her clit so that she exploded around him. Her scream had the dogs howling on the other side of the door.

"Holy hell. That was amazing, Rayna. You got a three-dog standing ovation."

"That's not funny, Jay." But she was laughing even as she moaned.

"Sorry about that, babe. I never dreamed the dogs would want in on this. Jay and I prefer to keep you all to ourselves."

"I'm not complaining." She panted as Jay crawled up the bed to sit next to her.

* * * *

She really wasn't. She'd never come like that and certainly never by someone else. It had always been her BOB or her fingers. That had been unbelievable. She felt like she was flying from the adrenaline rush it had given her.

Then Kenny crawled down between her legs and licked at her opening before he rolled on a condom and fitted his thick cock at her tiny slit. She felt herself tense up at the thought of how he could get it inside of her without it splitting her in two.

"Easy, sweetheart. You're tensing up. I promise it will feel great, but you've got to relax. If you're this worried about Kenny's dick, I have to wonder if you've had anything other than a pencil dick in your pretty pussy."

"Evidently not. You're both huge." She was sure her eyes were wide as lumberjack pancakes.

"Relax for me, Rayna. I promise not to hurt you."

Jay latched onto her nipple, pulling and nipping at it so that her attention was shifted there instead of on Kenny and what he was doing. The other man pinched her other nipple as he used his mouth on the first one.

The next thing she knew, Kenny had breached her opening and was slowly seesawing in and out of her. It felt so damn good she moaned. Why had she been so worried? He knew what he was doing. God, but he knew. She already felt the tight twinges of arousal that let her know she might climax if nothing changed.

Then Jay had his cock next to her mouth, and she saw that she was going to have another treat. She opened her mouth and licked over the bulbous head then across the slit at the top. He hissed as she slid her tongue across that slit several more times. She used one hand to grasp the base of his dick then slowly lifted her head to take more of him inside her mouth. She'd never been particularly good at giving head, but she wanted to make him feel good and worked at taking as much of him down her throat as she could handle before she gagged.

"Easy, Rayna. Don't choke yourself. You feel fucking amazing as it is. Just keep doing that. Yeah. Just like that." Jay's voice eased her worries as she sucked then swallowed then started over again.

She licked down the long stalk then circled the lip of his cockhead with the tip of her tongue. She loved the salty taste, which wasn't nearly as bad as she'd thought she'd remembered. Maybe it had been who she'd been with that made the difference. All she knew was that she didn't mind sucking Jay's cock one bit.

That complete thought flew away when Kenny began pumping in and out of her faster and a little harder. She could no longer control how she pleasured Jay. Now all she could do was hang on and enjoy the ride.

Kenny held her legs over his forearms as he thrust in and out of her wet cunt. She could feel his dick rubbing the most delicious way over her strained tissues. Her body ate him up and begged for more with each thrust of his hips driving his thick dick deeper and deeper inside of her.

She squeezed Jay's cock then lightly rolled his balls in her other hand. She needed to make him come before she lost control and accidentally bit him. Kenny had her so close to her own climax that it wouldn't take much to send her over.

"Yeah, Rayna. Just like that. Holy hell, that's good. Fuck, baby. I'm going to come. Hold up." She wouldn't release him. Instead, she swallowed all she could take, and the rest leaked from her lips around his dick.

He pulled out and collapsed next to her, his breath fast and loud. She would have smiled and basked in the fact that she'd made him feel good, but Kenny had her already so close to an orgasm she was fighting her own way to breathe. The next thing she knew, he tapped her sensitive clit a few times, and she came screaming once again. Her entire body felt light and floating before she landed back on the bed with her ears ringing and the chorus of dog howls letting her know it had been that good again.

Chapter Eleven

Rayna's eyes popped open as soon as she woke up. Where was she? The scents in the air and the feel of the bed wasn't her own. Then she remembered, with a blast of afterglow, the night before. She'd climaxed two times that had completely blown her mind. Hell, she'd made the dogs howl!

The fact that she'd had sex with two men at once worried her but not enough to dampen the heady feeling of bliss that battled the doubts and worries surrounding it all. She refused to feel trashy about what she'd done. They'd treated her like a princess and held her until she'd fallen asleep.

I've never felt so good after sex in my life and certainly not the next morning.

She sat up and looked around at the room and how warm it felt. A nudge at the door soon had three massive dogs climbing up on the bed around her. She couldn't help but giggle as the one called Chester nudged her with his boulder-sized head until she petted him and scratched behind his ears. The one called Roxie had taken her place on the other side of her and was resting her muzzle on Rayna's shoulder. Kojac had taken over her lap so that even if she wanted to get up, it so wasn't happening anytime soon.

"I should have known you three wouldn't stay out of trouble if I left you alone. Get off the bed and let Rayna breathe." Kenny clapped his hands, and the two mammoth animals climbed off the bed in slow motion, obviously not pleased about giving up their spots.

Rayna gave them each a last scratch and grinned at their mopey expressions

"Sorry about that. They don't follow directions as well as they should. I figure they just wanted to greet a fellow howler."

"That wasn't very nice," she said, letting her mouth form a frown.

"Hey! I'm basking in the knowledge that I helped give you that howl. It was awesome."

Rayna felt the blush heat up her neck and cheeks. She wanted to be angry with him but couldn't. She'd thoroughly enjoyed herself the night before.

"Come on. Time to get up and eat. Jay's fixed a breakfast feast fit for the French monarchy. I can't wait to eat, but he says we have to wait for the queen."

Rayna grinned but narrowed her eyes. "Something tells me that that door wasn't left cracked by mistake."

His complete look of innocence didn't make it with Rayna. His brows were too far lifted above his eyes. He'd done the deed. She was positive.

"Since I'm starved, I won't say anything to Jay about your little slip-up. I can smell the food, and my stomach is gnawing my insides." She climbed off the bed and was surprised when Kenny wrapped her in a huge fluffy green robe.

"Entertain at breakfast much?" she asked.

"Nope. You're the first, but when I saw this green robe the other day, I thought of you and had to get it."

That floored her. He'd bought a robe for her? Just for her.

Rayna led the way to the kitchen, despite not having remembered how to get there simply by following her nose. Kenny had been right. Jay had prepared a feast of massive proportions.

"Where did you get all of this? It can't have been in your pantry. It couldn't possibly hold all of this."

Jay chuckled. "I love to cook, so my pantry is overly big, and we have an industrial freezer and fridge. I hope you're hungry."

"Before I saw this, I would have said yes, I'm starved, but now I'm not sure a football team could eat all of this."

"Just eat what you want, babe. Most of it can be saved for later. I've gotten used to Jay's feasts. He tends to do that when he's happy."

"And I'm very happy this morning," Jay told her.

"See what I mean?" Kenny's eyes sparkled with that same happiness evident in Jay's eyes.

"I'll do my best. It all looks too good to touch though. Look at the pastries. They're beautiful." Rayna just shook her head.

If I were to spend much time with them, I'd be large as a barn.

Still, the way they played in bed, she might work most of it off. The giggle that escaped didn't seem to bother either man. They filled her plate with enough food for Chester then did the same with their own plates.

"Dig in, honey." Jay took a bite of bacon then shoveled a spoonful of fluffy eggs into his mouth.

"Here, try this." Kenny held a forkful of eggs with cheese and ham in front of her mouth.

Rayna closed her mouth around it and hummed her approval as soon as she tasted the delicious omelet.

"Mmmm. That's wonderful. Jay, I knew you could cook from the other day, but this is fabulous."

He just nodded and smiled as he ate. It didn't seem to bother him that she'd praised his cooking abilities.

"He knows. I've told him often enough. That's why I have to work out some. I'd end up a fat roly-poly vet if I didn't. Handling the small cat and dog isn't that hard, but trying to work around horses and cattle requires some strength and a normal-size body." Kenny shook his head at the other man. "I'm beginning to think that Jay might be trying to kill me in a roundabout way."

"Not a chance. I can't handle the zoo you have here. They won't mind me."

Rayna enjoyed their back and forth conversation almost as much as what she was putting her mouth. The man could cook. The fact that he was so good looking and damn good in bed made her wonder why they hadn't found their woman before now. What was the catch?

I better watch out, or I'll fall hard for them, only to find out there's some fatal flaw there somewhere.

She sure hoped not, but really. They were too good to be true.

"What are you looking so serious about over there?" Jay asked her between bites.

"Thinking about how dangerous you are for my waistline," she lied.

"Honey, you're perfect like you are, but if you gained a few pounds, I'd be all over that. Nothing like a curvy woman to stir me up." Jay reached across the table and squeezed her hand.

Yep, there's got to be a catch here somewhere. I just haven't found it yet.

After breakfast, of which the guys wouldn't allow her to help with the dishes, Rayna took a shower in the most decadent shower she'd ever been in. Two showerheads, side sprays, and a generous shelf that held her while she contemplated shaving her legs using one of their razors. In the end, she decided not to push that far and finally climbed out to dry off and wrap the comfy robe around her once more.

"There you are. Did you enjoy your shower?" Kenny asked.

"Loved it. It's dangerous though. I could have lived in it for the next twenty-four hours and shriveled into a raisin."

"Nah, we'd have come gotten you out after much longer. I brought you a pair of my sweats. They'll be too long, but should fit well enough to spend the day watching movies."

"Movies sound great. I felt all kinds of lazy after that breakfast."

"Jay tends to overcook a lot. Just eat what you want, and he won't feel slighted in the least. No reason to make yourself sick. We normally either take a short hike or watch movies or football on Sundays. Since you didn't bring anything to hike in, we figured movies would be nice."

"No football on, huh?" she asked, trying to keep from smiling.

"You got it." Kenny laughed. "It's spring training right now. Football will start again in a few months."

"Be still my heart." Her eyes crossed at the glee dripping in his voice.

"Hey, guys. Hurry up in there. I've got the movie ready to go." Jay's voice penetrated their bubble.

"I'm almost afraid of what he's chosen," Kenny said.

"Why?"

"He likes sappy love stories."

"My kind of guy."

* * * *

By the end of the second movie, Rayna was ready for a nap. Actually, she'd already started her nap prior to the end of the second movie.

"Someone's ready for bed again." Jay kissed her cheek. "I'll take her to bed, and you put up the DVDs."

Rayna heard him give the orders, but she couldn't for the life of her stop him from picking her up. She was too far-gone to walk, and she knew it. She decided it was a testament to the fact that he worked with wood that he could carry her without grunting. It was one more nail in her "I'm falling for them" coffin.

He laid her in the middle of the bed then climbed on next to her. When he pulled her back into his arms, she nearly lost it and fell asleep, but when Kenny climbed in with his back to her then pulled her hand over his waist to hold it, Rayna knew she felt complete.

The dream started out nice. She and the guys were at an outside party, dancing beneath the stars with tiny curtain lights surrounding the dance floor. No one else seemed interested in dancing, but the three of them danced as if it were the most natural thing in the world. Jay led, and she and Kenny circled with him as they enjoyed the entire square of dance space all to themselves.

The music stopped, and Kenny led them off to a table where they sipped champagne from tall plastic flutes. What was the occasion? She wondered. She couldn't remember why they were even there. Various people from her past stopped by the table to say hi and ask how she'd been. She was sure there had been two or three of her high school and college dates among the visitors.

"Wow. I see that they're still dating the same woman. I really thought they would've stopped that by now. Jay will never settle down. He likes variety too much. Don't let them break your heart." The strange woman whispered the last two sentences in her ear so the guys couldn't hear her.

When she stood back up, Rayna was surprised to see that she was fashionably skinny with long blonde hair and china-doll blue eyes. She shook her head and frowned. "Such a shame to fall in love only to get kicked to the curb a week later."

Rayna refused to listen to the bitter woman's words. The guys weren't like that. Were they? Had they dated around and had trouble committing to more than a few weeks with each woman? Was that the reason they were still single? Rayna prayed it wasn't true. She really liked them and could already feel her heart becoming involved.

Another woman stopped by the table and said just about the same thing. It worried Rayner more and more. Maybe she needed to stop and think this through. Two men as handsome and eligible as Jay and Kenny were shouldn't still be single.

Rayna woke with a no on her lips. Both men were sound asleep judging by their soft snores. She wanted to get up and dress and go home to think about her situation. Dreams didn't come true, but they often revealed what the innermost parts of a person didn't want to address. She needed to think about her relationship with Jay and Kenny. She liked them a little too much to let this end up in a broken heart. She'd had enough of them to recognize what led up to them. She needed to think.

Extracting her body from their tight hold wasn't going to happen without waking them up. She'd wait a little while then try again. It wouldn't be long before she'd have to get up to visit the bathroom anyway. The feel of Jay at her back, his warm body and the way his hand curved around her side felt so good. She couldn't help but enjoy snuggling up to Kenny's back with his scent of fresh earth and green grass. While he smelt of outdoors with a hint of antiseptic he probably used at work, Jay smelled of wood and shavings. It all made her think of home and happiness. She was in deep trouble already.

She waited as long as she could then pulled from Jay's arms to sit up.

"Hmm, what is it, honey?"

"Bathroom." She wiggled down the bed from between them.

"Okay," Jay said.

Kenny didn't wake up. Or at least she didn't think he did. Rayna slipped into the bathroom carrying her outfit from the day before. She quickly dressed and waited until she thought they'd have settled down into sleep once again. Then she slipped into the kitchen, where she realized that she didn't have a way home. It stopped her dead in her tracks.

Should I call a cab? It's a long way out here.

In the end, she settled for sitting on the couch and waiting for them to wake up. It wasn't the best scenario, but it was the only one she had right then. She'd never dreamed she would have spent the night with them or she would've insisted on bringing her own car. Rayna had never been in this type of situation before and felt helpless. The longer she sat there, the more anxious she became.

"Hey, babe. Are you okay?" Kenny walked into the living room in just his jeans with the top button open. She had to jerk her eyes upward.

"I'm fine," she lied. "I should probably be getting home. I have work tomorrow, and Patches and her family to tend to."

Kenny sat next to her and took her hand in his. "That's no problem. I'll finish dressing and take you home, but you should have woken us if you were ready. I hate that you've been sitting out here all alone."

"I didn't want to wake you up. You were both sleeping so deep."

"You mean you wanted to see how we'd take it waking up in each other's arms." He chuckled. "We just turned over and went back to sleep until I realized you weren't in the bed with us."

"Did you really?" She couldn't help the smile that rolled over her face.

"Yep." He pulled her hand so that she had to lean into him. "What's really wrong, Rayna? I can tell you have something on your mind."

"I think I'm worried this is all going a little fast."

"I understand, but I don't think it is. You fit with us so well, babe. I've never known Jay to be so taken with someone as he is with you. I think that we both met you and liked you without the other introducing you to each other. He liked you at the grocery store before he realized you were the same woman I'd met at the office."

"Why haven't you settled down before now?" she asked.

"We've never found the perfect woman for both of us. Until now. We truly care about you and want to see where this goes."

"I need to think about this, Kenny. It isn't just one of you. My heart could handle it if we broke up, but add in Jay and my heart might not be able to handle losing two of you in a week or three. It's all too much, too fast."

"So we hold off on anything too intimate and go slower. We can do that. You're that important to us, babe."

"Are you sure Jay will agree?"

"Yeah. He's gone over you just like I am. We'll do whatever it takes to satisfy you. We want you to be comfortable around us and feel good about dating us. We can work this out, Rayna."

"Okay. Do you mind taking me home?"

"Not at all. Let me finish dressing, and I'll be right back."

While she waited, Rayna replayed his words in her mind. He sounded like he was serious about wanting her to be happy with their relationship. Still, there were two of them, and she needed to hear Jay's thoughts on the subject.

Kenny returned in less than five minutes, dressed and smiling. "I'm ready."

The ride over to her little house didn't take long at all. There were few people on the road on the lazy late Sunday afternoon. When he cut the engine, he placed a hand on her leg. "I'll help you down."

She waited for him to walk around the truck and help her down then walk her to the door. She unlocked the door and turned to tell him thanks for the last twenty-four hours, only to find herself in a warm hug.

"Thanks for letting us spend the day with you today. I enjoyed the hell out of last night and today. One of us will call you later to say hi." Kenny kissed her on the forehead then squeezed her once more before opening the door for her. "Lock up behind you, babe."

Rayna did just that then leaned against the door while she waited to hear Kenny's truck start up and back out of her drive. Patches wove an intricate pattern through her legs as she stopped occasionally to sniff at her legs and feet.

"Yep, there were dogs and other cats where I've been. I promise. I love you most of all though." She reached down and petted the purring pussycat at her feet.

"I think I've fallen in love, Patches. What am I going to do?"

Chapter Twelve

Jay finished staining the last chair he was making for a client and stood back to look at it. He was proud of the work and felt he'd accomplished what they were wanting, but somehow it all felt off. He wasn't kidding himself. He knew why. Rayna. She occupied his mind all the time now. They'd spoken briefly Tuesday evening concerning going hiking Sunday morning. It was only Thursday, and already he was antsy to see her.

Kenny had told him that she felt pressured and was worried about how fast they were going. He'd agreed with his friend that they needed to step back and give her some space, but damn it was getting to him. He didn't want space. He wanted her there at their house every day and every night. Was it love?

I don't know for sure, but it's different from anything else I've ever felt. It probably is. I want her so much it's eating at me from the inside out.

He'd discussed part of what he was feeling with Kenny the night before. Kenny had said pretty much the same thing was going on with him. He wanted her with them. They needed to let her get used to being with both of them, but they also needed to be sure she knew they were serious and not just wanting to date her for the time being.

He and Kenny had talked quite a bit the last few nights, and both felt that they were falling for her and wanted to make their relationship permanent in the near future. Getting that point across to her without it sounding like a line wouldn't be easy in their current state.

Jay cleaned up and put away his tools. He didn't feel much like starting a new project, and it was nearly four anyway. He decided to cook dinner and maybe make a casserole to take to Rayna. She could warm it up anytime she wanted to.

By the time Kenny walked in at six that night, he had the shepherd's pies hot out of the oven. He'd let Rayna's cool off before wrapping it up to freeze if need be.

"Damn. Something smells good. What is it?" Kenny walked into their washroom and cleaned up before joining Jay in the kitchen.

"Shepherd's pie. I made an extra one to take to Rayna's house. I thought she might like to have something she could just thaw and warm up."

"Great idea. You should take it over to her tonight right after dinner."

"You can come, too," he said.

"Nah. You take her the pie. I've been talking to her every few days about the kittens. She's fallen in love with them."

"That's good, but hard when she needs to find homes for them."

"She'll be picky about who she lets them go to. That's good. They'll get great homes that way." Kenny leaned over the counter and sniffed the pie. "Can we eat now?"

Jay chuckled. "Sure. It's hot, so don't burn your mouth."

They each spooned up a nice portion to their plates then ate at the bar. Kenny handed Jay a beer and took one for himself. They ate in companionable silence.

"Are you having as much trouble with focusing as I'm having?" Jay finally asked his friend.

"Yeah, for the most part. The difference is that I have barking dogs and screeching cats to keep me focused. When I'm between patients, all I can think about is Rayna though."

"I baked the casserole just so I would have a reason to see her," Jay confessed.

"I know."

"Is that crazy or what?" Jay asked.

"It's not crazy. You're probably in love with her. I've about decided that I sure am. All I want to do is call and talk to her or go over there and just watch her work."

"We're both in trouble if she decides she doesn't want to see us anymore."

"I'm not even entertaining that thought." Kenny sighed.

"I'm trying not to, but I'm worried. That's why I'm going over there tonight. I have to see her, be sure she isn't getting over us or anything."

"Don't come on too strong, Jay. She'll back away for sure if you press too hard on this."

"I know. I'll be careful, but I have to see her." Jay shrugged. "I'm usually the one to back off first when we've been dating someone. This time I'm the one antsy about spending more time with her."

"It's why I think we're both in love with her. You took to her from the very beginning. I think the fact that you met her on your own, and liked her almost immediately, is why she's the one for us. Don't fuck it up, man."

"I won't."

As soon as they cleaned up, Jay wrapped up the shepherd's pie and settled it in an insulated carry-all. He set it on the floorboard of the truck and drove to Rayna's house across town. The little house was cute for a single woman. The flowers in front gave it a homey feel.

He hauled the carrier out of the truck and walked up to her front door. Jay hesitated for an instant then knocked on the door. Less than a minute later, Rayna opened the door with a surprised expression coloring her pretty face a soft shade of pink.

"Hi, Jay. I wasn't expecting you."

"I know. I'm sorry, but I didn't think to call. I cooked an extra shepherd's pie for dinner and thought you might like something to warm up sometime when you didn't feel like cooking." He thrust the dish at her feeling, decidedly uncomfortable.

Jay wasn't used to living things wrestling in his stomach, but they were sure there as he waited to hear Rayna's reaction to his sudden appearance on her doorstep.

"Well, come in. Should I let it cool some before I put it in the freezer?"

"No, it should be fine. I mostly used the carrier to make it easier to bring over." He stepped into the house and closed the door behind him.

"This was so nice of you, Jay. I really appreciate it. I hate cooking for myself. It seems like such a waste."

"This ought to do you for a couple of meals." Jay hesitated. For once in his life, he was at a loss for words. "Kenny said hi. He worked late and planned to make an early night of it."

Rayna smiled at him as she moved a few things around in her freezer to accommodate the casserole. She looked happy that he'd come by. Maybe she was feeling a little more comfortable about dating them both.

"Would you like some coffee or tea?" she asked.

"Coffee would great. If you don't mind."

"Not at all. Have a seat. I just signed off of work and was about to have a Diet Coke myself. I ate an early dinner and worked a little overtime."

Jay took a seat at the bar and watched her as she made coffee with one of those pod-type coffee makers. Then she pulled out a canned Diet Coke and set both it and the fresh-brewed coffee on the counter.

"Hope it's okay. I don't drink coffee but have some in case I decide to try a cup. Mostly I've used it for hot chocolate." Her smile pursed her lips as if she thought that was funny.

"I like fixing it on the stove with milk. When it gets cold, I'll have to make you some of mine. Kenny loves it."

"That would be nice."

The silence stretched as they sipped at their drinks and just stared at one another. Jay felt as if he could watch her, the way expressions crossed her face and how her smile was a little lopsided, all day long. It felt right. They felt right.

"Did you build anything interesting today?" she finally asked.

"Finished up some chairs, but I haven't started anything new yet. I'm still undecided about working on the library."

"Go for it. I'd love to be able to know that you made the shelves and counters when I visit there. I like to check out books sometimes that aren't on the e-book reader. I bet they'd be unique and gorgeous to look at."

Jay nodded. "Okay. I'll do it on one condition."

"What's that?"

"You help me with some of it. When you're not working, that is."

Rayna laughed. It went straight to his cock. "I can't build anything. I do good not to mess up tightening the knobs on my kitchen cabinets when they get loose."

"You can be my assistant and hand me tools. It's the only way I'll take on that big of a project. Hell, Kenny helps sometimes, and he's a klutz with tools."

"Okay then. If Kenny can help, I guess I can, too. When will you start?" she asked.

"They're almost finished with the framework. Once they have a roof over it and the walls up and finished, I'll start planning everything. That'll be in about a week to ten days I think. I'll let them know it's a go."

Rayna smiled and clapped her hands together. "I'm excited. I can't wait to get started."

Her enthusiasm had his mouth widening into a smile. Seeing her excited turned his insides to soupy mashed potatoes. He was besotted with her.

"I better be going and let you get on with your night. I need to clean up the kitchen, as well. We both know that Kenny isn't going to do it." He smiled.

"Thank you again for the food. I can't wait to try it tomorrow," she said.

He followed her to the door and didn't want to leave. Without waiting to think about it, Jay pulled her into his arms and kissed her. He pressed his mouth to hers then licked along her lower lip so that she opened to him without his pressing it. Her mouth was warm and wet and tasted so good. He wanted to explore and take, but he also knew that he was prone to push too fast. He slowly pulled back and smiled down at her.

"Goodnight, Rayna. Sweet dreams."

* * * *

She leaned back against the door with her head swimming at the kiss. She'd wanted more, so much more, but he'd been right to pull back. Rayna wasn't sure if she'd have been able to call a stop before things got out of hand or not. She wanted him. She wanted Kenny just as much. She knew that they came as a team and understood that there were other families like the one that they wanted, but it didn't make it any easier for her to accept in her head. Boy was her body on board though.

She ached for them.

Just the thought of what they could do in bed had her pussy growing moist as if it hadn't already done a rain dance after that kiss. Yeah, she wanted them so much it had her dreaming of them at night. Sometimes during the day she'd wanted to break away from work to pleasure herself to thoughts of them.

I've got it bad. I really like them. I think I'm falling in love with them, but it's too soon, right?

Rayna wasn't sure what to think about that. She'd never believed in love at first sight, but they'd been seeing each other a few weeks now. And there were two of them. How could she possibly love two men equally and fall for them at the same time?

She had way too many questions in her head to allow herself to think any further along those lines. Time would tell if there could be more between them than holding hands and kisses.

Lots of kisses.

She scowled. She needed to think of something besides those two men. She cleaned up the few dishes in the sink then wiped down the counters before heading to the bathroom to take a bath. She threw in some bath salts with lavender to help her rest when she lay down to sleep. The hot water soothed her achy muscles from sitting behind the desk all day.

She relaxed against the back of the tub and closed her eyes. It didn't surprise her that she started thinking of Kenny and Jay while she ran her hands over her wet breasts. She pinched at her nipples with thoughts of Jay sucking first one then the other while Kenny massaged her feet, leaving kisses up and down her legs. The double imagery had her pussy tingling before she knew it. Would it be the same way if they actually did it in person? Would she get this hot this fast with their actual hands and mouths on her?

Yes.

She was positive just from the few kisses they'd shared. Her body would sing for them. She just knew it. Already she felt close to orgasm just thinking about them. She lowered one hand to her pussy and began circling her clit with the tip of one finger while she pulled and plucked at her nipples. She had large breasts that ached for a man's hands.

She was so close. She imagined Jay spreading her legs and blowing his hot breath across her wet pussy lips then licking from one end to the other along her slit. It sent goosebumps all down her arms at the thought as she rubbed light circles over and around her clit. She dipped her fingers into her juices and spread them over the tight bundle of nerves.

She burned to climax. Her entire body felt strung as tight as a string on a harp. Rayna's body arched in the tub as she pinched her clit and pinched one nipple at the same time. The orgasm rolled over her in a soft rush of heat and pleasure. Her ears rang even as her heart pounded out a drumbeat of completion. She sagged in the tub and had to press her feet against the back of the tub to keep from going under.

I'd better get out before I end up drowning.

But she didn't want to move yet. She still swam dreamily in the afterglow of the mini orgasm thinking about two hunky men and what they could do just by being in her thoughts. She was ready to find out what being with them might be like.

Chapter Thirteen

"What do you think?" Kenny asked.

Rayna smiled. "I can do it. I think it will be fun."

"Well, let's get started. Jay, do you have all the food for the day?"

"Got it all packed. The water is in your pack. The tablecloth to eat on is in Rayna's pack."

"I hate that you're having to carry a pack, honey, but it will also help you remain balanced when we're walking on inclines. Just remember to lean forward some." Kenny picked up his and her backpacks. "Let's load up."

They climbed into the truck with the guys tossing the packs in the backseat. Once they were all buckled up, they drove thirty minutes to the trail Kenny wanted to use for the day. He'd picked it out because it wasn't one many people took, and it would give them more time to be together in some remote areas where he hoped they could spend a little more quality time.

They'd been dating for nearly six weeks now. The kittens had their six-week appointment the following Thursday for their checkup and shots. She'd be advertising them for adoption then, as well. Time had flown since they'd met her. All he could think about was her and how he could move a little faster. He and Jay were shivering with blue balls. Still, he'd rather not spook her by pressuring her for a more intimate relationship too soon.

They piled out of the truck and donned their packs before setting off at the trailhead. Kenny enjoyed pointing out the various indigenous plants as well as a couple of gray squirrels and the occasional bunny rabbit. She'd loved watching the bunny rabbits as they'd hopped across the trail in front of them.

They stopped twice for quick breaks and water. Then, at a little after noon, they reached the first of the secluded spots Kenny had planned to stop at. This one would do great for a light lunch.

"Here, let me get the pack off of you and spread out the cloth." Kenny helped her off with her pack then dropped his own next to it.

He unzipped hers and pulled out the blanket and spread it on the ground, anchoring it with rocks before helping Jay pull out their lunch.

The three of them sat cross-legged and ate ham and cheese sandwiches and chips while drinking water and talking about the trip so far.

"I was so surprised to see the first rabbit, but the second one really got me. She was so pretty with that huge fluffy cottontail. She had pretty ears, too."

"What makes you think it was a she? It could have been a male Jackrabbit," Kenny teased.

"It had to be a girl because she was so pretty. I'm saying it was a she." She smirked at him, daring him to argue with her.

"You win. It was a she. I'm not about to pick a fight with you." Kenny chuckled.

She beamed at him, making his cock jerk and his belly do a triple flip.

Kenny leaned over and cupped the back of her neck with one hand before lowering his mouth to hers for a kiss. He needed to taste her, or he was going to go crazy with need. Her lips were soft and warm and opened to him without prodding. It had started out as a gentle kiss, but he was so hungry for her that it soon raged like an inferno out of control. When she groaned into his mouth, he knew Jay had pressed against her from behind. Jay poked his hand to get him to move so he threaded his fingers through her hair and cupped the back of her head instead to give his friend access to her neck.

"You're so fucking sweet, Rayna. I'm going to need dentures if I keep tasting you."

Kenny dove back in for a repeat of the kiss then nipped his way down her jawline to her earlobe. He felt Jay on the opposite side of her neck as he licked then bit her neck and shoulder. When she moaned their names, he lost control and began shoving at her T-shirt to touch her skin. He ran both hands up her sides, enjoying the soft warmth of her skin.

"Let us love you, babe. We want to make you feel good."

"Please. I need you. I need you both." Her breathy answer had his dick pressing so hard against his jeans that it pinched when he moved.

"Let's get these clothes off of you." He started pulling at her shirt while Jay worked on her hiking boots.

By the time they had her nude, Kenny was sure he'd never get his jeans over his steel-hard cock. He reached behind his neck and grabbed a handful of his shirt to pull it over his head then tackled his own boots. There was no way he'd leave any of his clothes on when making love to her body. They'd all three get caught nude, not just their woman.

She must have thought about that when she spoke up. "What if someone comes?"

"We'll hear them on the trail below us first. We'll have time to scramble over behind the rocks if that happens. Don't worry. I picked this trail because it rarely gets used."

"You planned this, didn't you?" She clucked her tongue at him.

"I was being prepared like a boy scout."

"Were you a boy scout?" she asked as he and Jay finished undressing.

"I was, Jay wasn't."

"Jay? What were you doing instead of learning to be prepared?" she asked.

"Whittling. I loved to make things."

"Damn you look beautiful, Rayna. I can't wait to get between those lovely legs and lick your pussy." Kenny crawled over to kneel there. He spread her thighs wide and just stared down at the wet folds of her pussy lips.

Heaven.

"I'm going to play with your breasts, honey. I'm going to suck and lick your tits until you beg us for more. I love your breasts. They're the perfect size."

Kenny positioned himself so that he could slip his hands beneath her ass and hold her up to his mouth. She smelled like sex, and he knew she tasted like a wet dream. He leaned in and blew softly across her folds. She shivered, whining as he touched her here and there with just the tip of his tongue.

"Kenny." Her voice came out in an airy whisper.

"Easy, love. We've got you," Jay told her.

While his friend squeezed one breast with his hand and sucked on her other nipple, Kenny dragged his tongue from the bottom to the top of her glistening slit. Damn the taste of her was heady. He could feast off of her and never get enough.

Her whimpers heightened his arousal as he licked and sucked to his heart's content. She wiggled beneath him so that he had to put one hand on her belly to keep her still. He pushed one finger inside of her and searched for that sweet spot he knew would be there. He added a second finger, rubbing and thrusting until he found what he was looking for, and while he sucked on her clit, he stroked her to climax. She erupted around him, screaming his name to the top of the trail they were on. His friend covered her mouth in a kiss as he pulled back and dug through his pants pocket for the condom he'd stuffed there when they'd left.

Always be prepared.

He rolled it on then fitted her legs over his arms and guided his painfully hard dick into her sopping wet pussy. Even after her orgasm, she was a tight fit. He had to retreat and thrust several times to make it all the way inside of her.

"Fuck you're tight, babe. I'm not going to last long." He pulled out then pressed in, each thrust becoming harder and deeper. Her eyes held his as he thrust.

Then Jay touched his cock to her cheek. "Suck me, honey. I want to feel that hot, wet mouth swallow me.

She moaned and reached for him. It was all Kenny could do to hold on when her mouth took Jay's dick inside. This was what he'd wanted in life, to have a woman to share between them. Watching her climax while his partner got her off did it for him. Now he'd see her come with him inside of her.

Kenny kept his thrusts even and slow so that she could spend time sucking Jay's cock. She looked as if she were thoroughly enjoying herself. She had one hand working the man's balls while she squeezed and tongued his dick. Jay looked like he was in another world. He had no doubt it felt amazing being in her mouth. He caressed her cheek while holding on to a rock next to him.

Rayna began thrusting up with her pelvis, driving his dick deeper into her depths of wet, hot cunt. He could feel his balls burning as they drew up closer to his body. He could feel the urge to come like a rocket preparing to blast off. He needed Jay to hurry up, or he'd lose it while the other man's cock was inside of their woman's mouth. He couldn't let that happen. Kenny squeezed the base of his dick to slow things down, but it wasn't working as well as it should have. He needed to come.

"Hurry, man. I'm about to go."

"Her mouth is like wet silk, Kenny. Fucking wet silk." Jay threw back his head and roared as he came.

Rayna's throat convulsed around Jay's cock, and then he could see where some of the other man's semen escaped the corners of her mouth as she licked him clean then circled her tongue all around her mouth to get every drop. It was so fucking sexy.

He began releasing some of the control he had tried to keep in order to let Jay have his turn. Now he was thrusting in and out hard and deep. Fast and faster. His balls boiled with his seed, even as his cock strained. Kenny found Rayna's clit and began rubbing it with his thumb in hopes that he could send her over before he lost it.

She dug her fingers into Jay's hands as she threw back her head and called out his name. Her cunt squeezed him to the point of pain, and Kenny erupted, filling the condom and squeezing his ass to the point of pain. He felt like he had a fucking Charlie horse in his ass cheeks.

When he'd finished, all he could do was fall forward, catching himself with one hand before rolling onto his back and panting. He couldn't say anything for a good full minute.

"God, Rayna. That was unbelievable. I've never come that hard before. I think I pulled a muscle."

Her soft giggle sounded too muffled. He looked over and grinned. Jay had her head in his lap and was caressing her face.

"Come over here, babe. I want to hold you for a second. You can go back to Jay again in a minute."

She reached up and touched Jay's lips with a finger then rolled over to lay with her head on his arm. She felt good there. She looked good in Jay's lap, as well. This was perfect. It was time to tell her how he felt.

"You're amazing, you know that, right?"

"You and Jay are pretty darn amazing yourselves. I'm still floating."

He chuckled then grew serious. "I'm falling in love with you, Rayna. I may already be in love with you. Something about you completes me. Jay and I just can't spend enough time with you. We're always wanting more."

Jay lay down next to them so that his chest was against Rayna's side. "I already know that I love you. I usually back away first, but with you, there's no backing away. I want more. I want it all."

"I…I don't know what to say. I really like both of you. If I'm going to be honest, I'd say I'm falling for you, too, but I'm scared. This is so different." Rayna looked up into his eyes then over at Jay.

"We know it's too soon for more, but we needed to tell you what you mean to us."

"I don't understand where things go from here. I wasn't expecting this"—she used her hand to encompass what they'd done—"so soon."

"I know. But I don't regret one second of it. I wish we could stay just like this for the rest of the day, but we might better go ahead and get dressed."

Rayna giggled. "I'm surprised someone hasn't come up this way and caught us off guard."

"Could still happen. Get dressing, honey." Jay tickled her side then jumped up and grabbed her clothes.

Kenny couldn't stop the wide grin that stole over his face at the sight of the two most important people in his life playing around. Life was good and on the way to being perfect.

* * * *

Rayna couldn't stop thinking about what they'd done up on the trail earlier that day. Hell, she could still feel the effects, and a tremor would ripple over her sex at the mere thought of it. She'd never been so turned on in her life, and it hadn't been so much the slightly naughty, risqué location of their tryst but just that she'd had sex with two men again, and absolutely loved it.

Am I crazy or what? How can I love both of them? I do, though. I love them both so freaking much it scares me. What if one of them changes their mind?

She didn't want to have to think about that. She really didn't want to worry about it. Things were going so well. She was asking for trouble, that was all. Just because she was finally having a great time in her life and had two men who seemed to adore her just the way she was, extra pounds and all.

Everything felt so perfect, maybe too perfect. There had to be a big "but" somewhere in all of it. She just couldn't find it. Still, she could enjoy it while it lasted and prayed she didn't get hurt.

"You've got a pretty serious look there, babe. What's wrong?" Kenny helped her out of her pack when they'd returned to the truck.

"Nothing really. Just thinking."

"That's a lot of heavy nothing on your face. Don't keep anything from us. Honesty is the key to a relationship, especially one like we have," Jay told her.

"I'm just worried that it's too good. That something is going to jump out and ruin it all for me. For us. I really, really like you guys. I'm falling in love, and it scares me that I'm going to end up getting hurt."

"It's always a fear when you start thinking seriously about someone. Believe it or not, we feel the same way." Kenny started the truck. "That's why we have to keep communication open and not hold anything inside that can fester and get too large to overcome. Okay?"

"Okay. So you've been in a relationship like this before," she said.

Jay looked over at Kenny then back to her. "Yeah, we have. A few times, but they never progressed very far because one of us wasn't as into it like now. We knew pretty soon that she wasn't the woman for us."

"How did you know?" Rayna asked.

"Well, either Jay wouldn't be as excited to spend time with her as I was or the other way around. If you aren't thinking about the other person even when you're not together, then they're probably not the right one. Jay and I both can't stop thinking about you. When I think about something that happens at the clinic, the first thing I think about is telling you when I get off work."

Jay nodded. "I'm the same way. I'm working on a piece of furniture and thinking it would be great if you were there with me so I could show you how I lathe or ask you which color of chestnut you like best. I cook just so that I can bring it over to see you."

"I'm the same way, guys." She ran her hands over their thighs. "I have trouble concentrating at work and have to ask my customers to repeat what they said because I wasn't listening."

"See, we're all three into each other. It's right. We just need time to get to know each other better," Kenny said.

"How do you keep from feeling jealous? I still don't get that."

"We do get jealous, but not that kind of jealous. We'll always want to spend time alone with you, and that helps with any jealous feelings. I don't want to take you away from Kenny. I just can't wait until my turn to hold you," Jay told her.

"I love seeing you in Jay's arms. I like watching your face when he makes you happy, when he makes you come. I want to be able to watch you fall apart when he fucks that sweet pussy of yours. I'll get my time, and he'll get to watch you like I did. It's a huge turn-on for me." Kenny glanced over at her so that she could see the seriousness in his eyes.

"I guess it's just going to take time for me to feel completely comfortable that this will work. I know it's worked for other couples, but I need to feel it myself to believe it."

"We get that, and we've got time, Rayna. We've got lots of time for you to become comfortable with it." Kenny smiled. "I'm not saying we don't want you as ours right this minute, but we can wait for you to be ready."

"I can't believe we actually had sex outside on a mountain!" She dissolved into a fit of giggles. "Talk about crazy."

"Listen to her. She's more excited about that than she is about dating two men at one time." Kenny reached over and pulled her head closer so that he could kiss her on the nose.

Rayna felt the happiest she'd felt in as long as she could remember. Yeah, life was good.

Chapter Fourteen

Rayna hated grocery shopping. She just didn't like dealing with the crowds and normally did hers at night. Today, however, she was completely out of Diet Coke, milk, and eggs, so she didn't want to wait until later to go. She grabbed a cart and headed for the Diet Coke first.

"I guess you're trying to lose some weight now that you're dating Kenny and Jay. I'd be, too, if I were you. They don't stick long with any particular woman." The blond with shoulder-length hair stared at her with one hand on her cart and the other on her hip.

"I beg your pardon? I don't think I know you, so how would you know me?" Rayna felt the first stirrings of unease.

"Oh, everyone in town knows you're dating those two. It's a running joke on how long it takes for Jay to get tired of a woman so that Kenny has to call it off. I figure you've another two weeks, and then they'll be saying bye to you, as well. Bet Jay is already backing away, right?"

"You don't know anything about us. I'd appreciate it if you'd keep your thoughts to yourself." Rayna pushed her cart in the opposite direction.

"I'm Tanya, by the way. They lasted the longest with me. You'll see."

Rayna headed across the store to where the eggs and milk were. She wanted out of there as soon as possible. The woman's words had unnerved her. She was so pretty, so perfect with a perfect body. Why would they have stopped seeing her when she was that pretty? What did that say for Rayna? She was a few pounds overweight and lacked hair that would always look nice no matter how you styled it. What did the guys see in her anyway?

Stop it. I can't go second-guessing anything. They're with me now, and they haven't shown any hints that they're tired of me. I have to trust them.

Could she trust them?

Yes. She could. They'd shown no hint that they were growing tired of their relationship. If anything, they'd acted like they wanted it to last forever. She wasn't going to let the bitchy blond ruin her happiness.

She was taking her kittens to see Kenny that afternoon. She couldn't wait to see him again. It would go a long way to making her feel better, she was sure.

At two p.m., Rayna carried momma and the kittens in their carrier inside the veterinarian clinic and signed in. The girl at the desk looked harried but smiled and cooed over the playful kittens chewing and jumping on their patient momma.

"Her name is Patches. We have a two-fifteen appointment," she told the woman.

"It might be a little longer. We've had a very busy morning, and Doc Kenny hasn't even stopped for lunch."

"Goodness. Should I come back?"

"No, no. He'll see you as soon as he can."

Rayna took a seat on an old church bench and set the carrier next to her so that she could watch the kittens' antics. Patches was such a good momma. She was going to hate separating them from her. The momma cat had come a long way and had put on a good bit of weight after her ordeal.

It was close to two thirty before she was called to the back. The vet tech gave her a strained smile. "Sorry it took so long."

"No problem. I hear you had a busy morning."

"Yeah. We're catching back up though. The doc will be with you in a few minutes."

Rayna stood at the table where the carrier was siting, waiting for Kenny. She heard some soft murmurs outside the door of the vet's office. At first she didn't understand them. Then they got a little louder.

"Casey, I'm sorry, but I'm really busy right now." Kenny's voice sounded harried.

"You always have time for me, Kenny. I haven't talked to you in a while and wanted to see if you wanted to come by tonight for dinner."

"Thanks for the offer, but I'm too busy. I need to go."

"You always have time for me. Just stop by for drinks then." Casey wasn't taking no for an answer the way Rayna heard it.

"Look, maybe another day. I've got to go." With that, her door opened and Kenny walked through.

Rayner saw just a hint of the other woman, who had a svelte body and long brown hair. Then the door closed behind Kenny.

"Hey, Rayna. I'm so sorry for the wait. We've been swamped, and I had an emergency early on." He washed his hands and dried them then turned to look in the cage. "They look great. You've taken good care of them."

"Patches did all the work." She felt uncomfortable at having overheard the outside conversation.

"Let's take a look at them." He pulled out each kitten and weighed them all before giving them their injections. "They all look healthy and are a good weight for six weeks."

"They're so playful, and Patches lets them walk all over her and chew on her tail and ears without batting an eye."

"I'm going to weigh her and see where we stand on getting her fixed." Kenny set Patches on the scales then whistled. "She's up to six and a half pounds. That's pretty good for her size. We can look at fixing her in the next two to three weeks. You can make an appointment for that on the way out."

"Great. Thanks so much. I took pictures of the kittens. Can I post them on your bulletin board with my number?"

"Yeah, that will be fine. I hate to run, but I need to keep moving. I'll talk to you later, Rayna."

His briskness bothered her a bit, but then she told herself that he was behind and had had an emergency that morning. She couldn't expect him to spend extra time with her just because they were seeing each other. It bothered her though.

After making an appointment for Patches to be spayed in three weeks, Rayna put up the pictures and descriptions of her kittens along with her number in order to find good homes for them. Just as she was leaving, she heard the voice of that woman from earlier asking to speak to Kenny again. Rayna refused to let jealous feelings eat at her and hurried through the door.

After she'd resettled Patches and her kittens at home, Rayna logged back into work. She couldn't help thinking about everything that had happened that day, and doubts began to creep into her head. Were they growing tired of her? Why hadn't Kenny told the other woman that he wasn't interested or that he was seeing someone? That should have put an end to her harassing him if he had. Rayna had to work at concentrating on work and knew she hadn't given her best that day by the time she logged out for the night. That wasn't like her. She needed to put her fears to rest.

She decided to surprise Jay and run by to say hi and find out what he was working on. He liked it when she stopped by to see his latest piece.

Twenty minutes later, she knocked at the door to his shop and waited for him to answer. When he did, he looked just as harried as Kenny had earlier.

"Rayna. Um, I wasn't expecting you." He just stood there then opened the door wider. "Come on in."

"I'm sorry. Did I catch you at a bad time?" Those niggling doubts began to fester like an open wound deep inside of her.

"No. I'm just having some trouble with one of the shelves I'm building for someone. She came by and wanted some changes made to it that are giving me fits."

Rayna walked over to the bookcase and thought it looked amazing with all the scrollwork at the top. How could someone possibly have a problem with it? That was when she saw the two glasses of wine, along with an empty bottle, sitting on his desk. She looked from that to him, and his face turned a light red until even the tips of his ears were red.

"She brought the wine to celebrate the bookshelf and desk I'm building for her," he quickly explained. Jay quickly tossed the empty wine bottle in the trash and moved the glasses to the sink across the room.

"I took Patches and the kittens to Kenny today for their six-week checkup and shots. Patches is getting fixed in about three weeks."

"That's great. I know you've loved having them, but they need their own homes. Did you put up their pictures on the board there?" he asked as he picked up a chisel.

"I did. It's going to be hard to say good-bye, but it's for the best. I'm still thinking of keeping one of the kittens so Patches has a companion, but I'm not sure yet."

She watched as Jay started working on the shelf again. He didn't seem to be interested in hearing about Patches or her kittens. She wasn't used to him focusing on something other than her when she was around him.

"Maybe I should go. You look really busy."

He stopped to look back at her. "Yeah, I'm sorry. This piece really has me determined to get it right."

"Sure. I'll see myself out. Bye, Jay." She turned back to the door and walked over then looked over her shoulder to say bye again when he didn't say anything, only to find him already working on the shelf not paying any attention to her.

Rayna opened the door and walked back to her car. The blond woman's words came back to haunt her. Jay seemed to be pulling back. Maybe they had just wanted to have sex with her, and then, when it was over, they weren't as interested. Maybe she hadn't been as good as they expected, and now they were looking elsewhere.

Those thoughts plagued her all the way home. The idea that she'd given herself to them believing that they were serious about her started an ache deep in her gut. It twisted and rolled until she wasn't surely she'd make it back home before she got sick.

The moment she walked through the door, Rayna headed for the bathroom and threw up. She was making herself sick thinking about all of it. Why would they treat her that way unless they were growing tired of her? She wouldn't allow them to break her heart any more than it already was. Rayna would keep to herself and stop chasing after them. It was obvious they didn't want to be caught.

* * * *

"Have you talked to Rayna today?" Kenny asked several days later.

"No. What about you?" Jay asked.

"No. I haven't seen or heard from her since she brought the kittens by for their checkup. I figured she'd at least call and talk to you. Something's up."

"She's probably just busy since she took off from work to bring Patches and the kittens to you the other day. She's probably working extra to catch up."

"Yeah, and I was completely behind after having spent the morning working on the dog that was brought in with his collar embedded in his skin. That took up a lot of my time, so she was there a lot longer than she should have been. You're probably right." Kenny thought back to that day. He'd been kind of brisk with her now that he thought about it. The entire fiasco with the dog had pissed him off.

Surely he hadn't taken it out on all of his customers, especially Rayna.

"Didn't you say she stopped by that night before I made it home?" he asked Jay.

"Yeah. I was really busy trying to get Marsha's bookcase right. She'd wanted a lighter scrollwork than what I'd put on it, so I had to rework it."

"So we were both a little brisk with her. Do you think that's why we haven't heard from her? I mean just because we're a little busy sometimes she shouldn't get her feelings hurt over that." Kenny couldn't believe it was that simple.

"If she gets upset over every little thing, it won't be a smooth relationship. I get testy sometimes when I have a problem with a piece, but I didn't bite her head off or anything, but I guess she doesn't know us that well yet."

Kenny nodded but still wasn't sure that was the problem. He thought about calling her and asking her out for coffee the next day but remembered he had a long morning of surgeries and wouldn't be free until well after lunch. He needed to make sure she was okay. They hadn't talked about doing anything that weekend. Now was a good time to make plans.

"Want to go hiking again on Saturday?" he asked his friend.

"I don't think I can Saturday. I've got to finish the desk and get it out of my shop before I burn it. I've never had so much trouble with a piece before." Jay ran a hand over his face.

"How about Saturday night we grill out and watch a movie," Kenny suggested.

"I like that idea. I should have the desk finished by then."

"I'll call her and set it up. I miss her."

"Yeah, me, too. I started to call her a couple of times but didn't want to sound desperate, you know?"

"We dropped the ball this week though. Neither one of us had time for her and that has to stop. We can't keep up a relationship if we let other things get in the way." Jay walked out of the kitchen into the living room.

Kenny pulled out his phone to call. It went to voice mail. He listened to her message then left one of his own.

"Hey, Rayna. Sorry we haven't called. We should have. We wanted to see if you were free Saturday night to cook out on the grill then maybe watch a movie. Call back when you have time." He ended the call and wondered what she was doing that she hadn't answered her cell.

I bet she was in the bathroom or was taking the trash out or something.

Still, it wasn't like her to not have her phone on her or to call right back. He checked his watch and saw that it had been only two minutes. What was wrong with him? He didn't usually get this worried over a missed call.

I feel guilty about how I treated her the other day.

He hadn't been rude or anything, but he'd brushed her off and hurried on to his next patient. She might have had questions about Patches' upcoming surgery. He hadn't treated his other patients that way. He'd felt comfortable that he'd see her again soon and make it up to her. Now she wasn't answering her phone. He checked his watch again. Three minutes. Sheesh.

"What did she say?" Jay asked when he returned to the kitchen.

"She didn't answer, so I left a message on her voice mail."

"That's not like her. She always answers the phone."

"Yeah, I know."

Jay checked his watch. "It's only seven. She can't be in bed. Let's ride over and check on her."

"That's a good idea. We can go in my truck. I know you've probably got yours set up to move the desk and bookcase when you finish them."

"Yeah."

Kenny and Jay climbed into Kenny's truck and drove over to Rayna's house. The light in the front part of the house was on, so they figured sure she was still up. They got out then walked up to the door, where Kenny knocked. A few seconds later they heard someone walking toward the front door. Rayna opened the door with surprise on her face.

"Um, hey, guys."

"We came over to see how you were. You didn't answer your phone, so we were a little worried," Kenny told her.

She stood there with the door half closed for a second before she answered them.

"Sorry. I left my phone in my office and hadn't thought about it. Um, do you want to come in?" she asked.

"Yeah, thanks." Jay walked in once she opened the door wider. Kenny followed him.

"Are you feeling okay?" Kenny asked.

"Yeah. I'm fine. Why?"

"Well, we hadn't heard from you since I saw you with Patches and the kittens," Kenny said.

"I guess I hadn't realized it had been so long. I've been super busy with work, and then just so tired I've crashed early each night. Plus, I didn't want to bother you guys. I know how busy you are."

"We're never too busy to make time for you, Rayna. If we act like we are, hit us over the head and remind us. I've missed you." Kenny reached for her.

Rayna hesitated for a few seconds then let him enfold her in his arms. She felt stiff at first but relaxed after a few brief seconds. She felt so damn right in his arms. Why were they at odds with each other? What had happened? Surely it wasn't just that they'd be short with her? She didn't strike him as a needy person who wanted to be first and foremost in their minds at all times. Sure, they thought about her all the time, but they had to work some, as well.

"I know I was a little harried the other day when you brought Patches in, but I didn't mean to be. Forgive me?" he asked.

"Of course. You're going to be busy or have a bad day from time to time. I understand that. I have those, too."

Jay pulled her out of Kenny's arms and hugged her. "I'm sorry I ignored you the other day, as well. I was so aggravated about having to rework that shelf that I took it out on you. Forgive me?"

"Of course. I know both of you have jobs just like I do. I shouldn't have been hurt, but I was because I've heard that, by a couple of months, you start to pull away from whomever you're dating and start seeing other people. I was scared that I was losing you."

"Oh, I see. The wine glasses probably didn't help that idea, did it? The project's owner brought it by when she told me she wanted to change a design on the piece I was working on. It didn't make a difference with me, though," Jay said.

"No, they didn't. I've been told that you usually get bored first. I felt like you'd gotten bored with me and were looking for the next woman to court. It hurt."

"I'm so sorry, Rayna. I'm not trying to pull away. Just the opposite. I love you. I don't want to lose you, but we let life get in the way, and that won't happen again. I don't want to even think about losing you." Jay kissed her.

Kenny pulled her back from Jay and kissed her. Savoring the taste of her and deepening it the second she opened her mouth to him. He loved the taste of her and how responsive she was to them. When he pulled back, her eyes were heavy-lidded and dark with emotion.

"I love you, Rayna. I don't want you to ever forget that."

He kissed her again, running his arms up and down her back as he did. Then he cupped her ass and squeezed her ample hips. He loved being able to squeeze her. No bones bruising him with her. Why they'd ever dated skinny women he didn't know. He loved how she felt in his arms and wanted to explore her body once again.

"God, you turn us on." Jay's words from behind her mimicked the thoughts in his head.

"You guys drive me crazy. I love you both. I was so afraid that I was losing you. I hadn't known that you'd dated most of the town's single women and grown tired of them. When I found out, I was scared that was happening with me."

"I'm ashamed of that fact, but we were looking for our perfect woman and couldn't find her. We've found her with you, Rayna. We want to make our relationship permanent. Will you marry us?" Kenny asked.

Chapter Fifteen

Rayna gasped. "Really? You want to marry me?"

"Yes. It's sort of spur of the moment, so we don't have the ring with us, but we don't want you to ever doubt us again."

Rayna felt her head spin even as her stomach fought a battle inside of her. They wanted to marry her. Rayna. They loved her and wanted to be with her forever. It brought tears to her eyes as she nodded.

"Yes. I'll marry you. I can't believe it. I was so worried you wanted to end things."

"Where's your bedroom, babe? We're going to celebrate by driving you crazy and making love." Kenny picked her up so that she squealed for him to put her down.

"I'm too heavy, Kenny. You'll hurt yourself."

"Honey. You don't weigh a thing. I pick up heavy dogs and turn over cows all the time. Let me worry about my health." He kissed her then followed her directions to the back of the house where her bedroom was.

She was so glad she'd made up the bed and picked up some that morning. Kenny laid her on the bed, and then he and Jay started undressing in front of her. Rayna watched with anticipation as each piece of clothing came off and was discarded on the floor without a thought. Once they were both completely nude, Rayna gave them a show of slowly removing her clothes, as well.

When she got to her bra and panties, Jay took over by unhooking the bra and tossing it to the floor while Kenny pulled down her lace panties, letting them drop, as well. Both men lay down next to her and began caressing and kissing her all over. When they both took a nipple into their mouths, Rayna threw back her head and gasped for air. Two mouths and two sets of hands on her drove her crazy. She couldn't concentrate on any one person.

"Please. I need you. Don't tease me anymore, guys. I need you inside of me."

"We've got you, babe. We'll take really good care of you." Kenny's raspy voice in her ear had her pussy fluttering even as her stomach flipped like a stack of flapjacks.

Jay kissed and licked his way down her belly, pausing at the juncture of her thighs and belly to tease her with tickling licks that had her bucking at the sensation. He chuckled before settling between her legs. He spread them wide to fit his broad shoulders then spread her pussy lips and licked her like a lollipop. His tongue stirred up her nerve endings so that she attempted to move her hips to get his tongue on her clit. He chuckled against her pussy slit. Then he circled her clit with the tip of his tongue.

"Jay! Please. Don't tease me. I need you."

Kenny was driving her crazy with his mouth moving from one breast to the other then up her neck to nip at her neck, her ear lobe. He was driving her insane. She wanted to hold him at her breast, but he felt too good all over to limit his movement.

Jay regained her attention when he entered her with one finger and began to lap at her pussy as if he had an ice cream cone that was melting and he wanted to keep it from dripping. When he let his tongue run over her clit, she exploded without realizing she was going to. He held her still with one arm across her pelvis as he sucked and licked her juices clean.

"Damn, Rayna. That was so fucking hot. You came all over my face. I couldn't get enough of you."

"I've never done that before. Oh. My. God. That was unbelievable." Rayna felt too good to be embarrassed. Her head was spinning with a wave of sound buzzing in her ears.

"Roll over on top of Kenny, honey. That's it. Straddle him." Jay's words in her ears as she slid down onto Kenny's long, hard cock had her insides tightening. "Ride him for me, Rayna."

She slowly rose up on her knees then slid back down Kenny's slick dick. She couldn't believe how his thick dick filled her to near bursting. If she hadn't been so wet from her climax, Rayna wasn't sure she'd have been able to fit him inside of her like this. When she sat flush with her pussy against his pelvis, she swore she could feel him touching her throat. It was too much. It wasn't nearly enough.

"Please, I need more. Help me, Kenny."

"Don't worry. We're going to take care of you. Lean toward me, Rayna." Kenny wrapped his arms around her once she'd leaned against his chest.

She felt something cold and slippery run down her ass cheeks. She looked back over her shoulder the best that she could and saw that Jay had poured some of her baby oil down her ass. It finally dawned on her that they were going to take her together. That meant Jay was going to fuck her in the ass. She couldn't help the trepidation that poured over her. She was sure it would hurt, but she wanted them both.

"Just relax and let us take care of you. We won't hurt you, babe. If you say stop, we stop." Kenny's voice soothed her worries.

She felt Jay's finger breach her ass. He slid it in and out several times before adding more oil and a second finger. It burned, but didn't hurt. She felt full, and the first inklings of pressure began to build inside of her.

Jay added more oil then slowly fitted three fingers inside of her. The burn was intense, and she almost asked him to stop, but after another few seconds, she stretched enough that it didn't hurt anymore. He thrust in and out with the three fingers, spreading them and closing them to stimulate her ass muscles to relax. Then he removed them, and she felt his cockhead pressing inward.

"Oh God."

"Easy, Rayna. Just tell us if it's too much."

The burn Jay's dick caused was much more than his fingers had. She felt as if her throat would close up as he pushed through the tight ring of muscle that resisted him. Once he was inside of her, she relaxed, letting out a whimper that had him stopping.

"Rayna? Do I need to stop?"

"No. Don't stop." She wanted to feel him move inside of her. She needed, something, anything.

He pushed deeper then pulled back and thrust again. Kenny pulled out as Jay pushed in, and then they each did the opposite. Over and over they moved inside of her, driving her higher and higher until she was afraid of falling. Each rasp of Jay's cock in her ass and every thrust of Kenny's dick into her pussy shoved her higher and higher up some invisible ladder so that she was sure when she fell it would kill her.

They continued their sexy dance, in and out, up and down. Rayna felt her desire sharpen and her orgasm building. She couldn't possibly last much longer. Small whimpers escaped her lips as the guys' thrusts and retreats lost their rhythm as they, too were getting closer and closer to their release.

"Hurry," she croaked out. "Please, I need more."

They increased their movements, but it wasn't until Kenny pressed a hand between them to rub her clit that Rayna's orgasm poured over her, sending her screaming headlong into an inferno of heat and pleasure that she didn't think would ever release her.

She felt Kenny fill her with his cum even as Jay erupted inside her ass. Heat burned as he slowly pulled free of her back hole and collapsed next to her and Kenny. Rayna didn't know how Kenny could breathe since she was having a hell of a time catching her breath lying on top of him.

"Dear Lord, guys. I'm dying. Can't catch my breath."

Kenny rolled her over toward Jay so that they both had more lung space to catch their breaths.

"That was so good. God, babe. You strangled me with your hot little cunt. I've never felt closer to passing out like I did this time." Kenny brushed her hair from her face. "I love you, Rayna. More than you can ever know."

Jay kissed the back of her neck after lifting her hair. He trailed kisses around to her shoulder, where he nipped her. "You've killed me. I'm yours, honey. All yours."

She sighed, happier than she'd ever felt before. "I love you both, too. I think I'm going to take a nap now."

Jay chuckled. "I'm going to clean up. I'll be right back."

Rayna groaned when the bed dipped as he got up. Kenny continued petting her, running his hand up and down her back, over her hair to softly squeeze her ass cheek. Then Jay was back and cleaning her there. He worked carefully so as not to hurt her, but she felt a lot better once he'd finished. Then he curled up to her back and kissed her shoulder again.

"Rayna. I love you with all my heart. I can't wait to get our ring on your finger, honey. I want everyone to know that you belong to us and we belong to you."

"This feels so right. I never would have thought I'd date two men, much less marry them. You're the best thing that's ever happened to me. I'll be your wife and make sure you never regret asking me."

"And we'll make sure to never let you wonder how we feel about you," Jay told her.

"I hope you have room for Patches in your zoo," she teased.

"There's room for you and Patches in our home and our hearts forever," Kenny said.

THE END

WWW.MARLAMONROE.COM

Siren Publishing, Inc.
www.SirenPublishing.com